BEYOND THE WHEEL OF HISTORY

Iskar D'Abrel

SKA
LIUM

Beyond the Wheel of History is a work of fiction. Names, characters, places and incidents either are the product of the author's imagination or are used fictitiously. Any resemblance to actual persons, living or dead, or locales is entirely coincidental.

2018 Skalium Press Paperback Edition

Copyright © 2018 by Iskar D'Abrel

All rights reserved.

Published in the United States by Skalium Press, Irvine, California.

ISBN 978-0-996836-2-0 (trade paperback).

Printed in the United States of America on acid-free paper.

www.iskardabrel.com

1st edition.

May this book nourish the seeds of humanity and spirituality in all of us.

CHAPTER ONE

SUMMIT ON THE WHEEL OF HISTORY

Present time.

In a busy business area of a large, modern city, Jeremy, a thirty or so year old man, entered a toy store. An attractive, young saleswoman checked him out from head to toe, thinking that such a handsome man, so well-built and dressed, was a rare sight.

"Good afternoon." She said smiling, looking him in the eyes.

"Hello." He, too, smiled at her and walked towards a basket with teddy bears.

"Can I help you decide?" She asked, noticing the uncertainty on his face.

"Well, I hope you can... It's difficult to decide; they are all so adorable."

"Aren't they? Let's see . . . You won't make a mistake if you go with this one." She was convinced. But she saw that he still wasn't.

"Trust my choice," she said. "You won't regret it."

"All right. It's settled then. Thanks for saving me here," he said with relief, starting to like her choice more and more.

"What cologne are you wearing?" she asked. I love it. I thought I was an expert on colognes, but yours . . . I can't fit it into any category."

"Oh that. Haha. I'm in the fragrance industry. That tall building across the street is the company I work for. A few days ago I mixed something, a bit of this, a bit of that, and it turned out as it did. I am glad you like it."

"How did you end up in the fragrance industry? Perhaps you have some exotic story to tell me," she anticipated.

"No, not really. It's the smell of human history... wars, blood, destruction, suffering. Fragrances help me smell less of that. How did *you* end up in a toy store? What's your story?"

"This job pays the bills. I am a graduate student in Philosophy." She said.

"How impressive! What's your thesis about?"

"The library of Alexandria and Ptolemy's reasons for building it."

"Ah yes, I am familiar. The library burned... thousands of priceless scrolls devoured by a merciless fire. Wooden shelves, desks, walls, everything that made it great lost to relentless flames... All that smoke—dark, impenetrable, suffocating. Nostrils consumed with the smell of unstoppable annihilation of classical gems. Human species set back centuries."

"You depict it so well, as if you were there. What a talented storyteller you are, did you know that? But, yes. Immeasurable ancient knowledge irreversibly lost. Very depressing, indeed," she admitted.

"What's your name?" Jeremy asked.

"Ashley, and yours?" She extended her hand.

"Jeremy. Nice to meet you." He answered shaking her hand.

"Nice to meet you too. So, have you named your cologne? She inquired. "I'll make sure to get it."

"It doesn't have a name yet, but, it will be 'Ashley,' after you." He smiled, and she smiled back. "It should come out in six months; you can get it then for your significant other," he added.

"Well, Jeremy, your cologne will show up in stores faster than Mr. Right in my life," She confessed. "Right now, a significant other is missing in action."

"I'm sure you'll soon make someone happy. Many wonderful men would feel lucky to know an educated, kind, helpful and interesting person like you." This was a compliment that she couldn't easily forget.

"Perhaps I'll make *you* happy, Jeremy." She gave him a wink, an unmistakable sign that she was interested. He did not have a ring on his finger, so she thought he was single perhaps. "You know, we could make amazing fragrances together," she flirted.

"Well, if I were into dating right now, it would be something like that. But... I wish you a great day and a wonderful romance in the future. You deserve that. Goodbye Ashley." He smiled at her and left the store.

Ashley did not wait a second, and dialed a number on her cell.

"Dee, you'll never guess who just left my store. A real gentleman: kind, educated, gorgeous, early thirties, tall, dark hair, blue eyes, perfect body, dressed amazingly, perfect shoes. Most importantly, he didn't compliment me on my looks, only my personality, which, you know, is rare... very rare in this day and age. Usually they start with how great our hair is or how pretty we are.

Often their gaze is on our chest, right? But, this guy... He was perfection, in my book. A 10+. I hope he..."

"Let me tell you, my dear," Dee interrupted. "There must be something so wrong about your Mr. Perfect. I bet you he's a serial killer or worse—a mass murderer. He's only pretending to be that wonderful. That's my free diagnosis. You're fortunate that he left. I hope he ain't coming back. For your own sake."

"Haha. You and your conspiracy theories. He may be just a perfect gentleman, and that's all."

Jeremy crossed the street, using the stairs to reach the tall bank building. A brand new prospering branch in the very center of the downtown with a lot of people inside.

"Reason for your visit?" the security guard at the entrance, asked Jeremy, inspecting his ID.

"Meeting with the owner," Jeremy said.

"Your name is on the list. Please put your bag over there and step into the scanner." Jeremy did as he was told.

Leaving the scanner, he reclaimed his bag and went into the elevator. Several other people walked in with him. He was the only one pressing the button for the top floor. Exiting, he went right through a wide hallway. In the distance, in front of him, there was a large and opaque spherical structure connecting the floor and the ceiling. On the left and right walls of the hallway, were white reliefs of ancient battles. In front of the walls were ancient sculptures which, as usual, had lost their arms, legs, and noses long ago.

The floor below Jeremy was a mosaic, depicting a priest in black clothes. The priest's mouth was open and there was dark smoke coming out of it. Several steps later, the mosaic depicted a physician treating a patient on a bed, next was a gladiator, after that, a man at a table with a jar of money, perhaps a merchant or a banker, then there was a female lawyer in a courtroom, and finally a queen with a crown sitting on a throne. But, there was something that all of the faces had in common—an opened mouth from which dark smoke arose. Jeremy did not pay attention to any of it; it was as if he had been here many times before. He was focused on getting to the opaque sphere in the middle.

The opaque stone structure was right in front of him now. It had a myriad of symbols cast in it—Mayan, Druid, Egyptian, Sumerian. Following the curvature of the sphere, he reached the opposite side. There, among numerous symbols, was a relief of a female face with an opened mouth. Jeremy lowered his head towards her mouth and whispered into the opening "He-re-mi-on," with a long exhalation. From his mouth, dark, wavy smoke appeared, resembling black ink dropped into water. The smoke was sucked into the sculpture's mouth, and then, an ultraviolet black light illuminated the smoke, identifying it, and shortly after, the smoke returned from the opening straight into Jeremy's mouth that sucked it in. The sculpture's head separated vertically in the middle, opening the door of the object. It was an elevator. He stepped in, pressed a button and began moving upwards. On the walls of the elevator were Renaissance and Baroque paintings.

Each painting depicted disturbing emotions. One by Rubens, showed terrified, hopeless women, being kidnapped by merciless, distant, intimidating horsemen; next to it was a painting by Bruegel, showing ferocious skeletons with sticks and scythes, torturing and murdering terrified people; on the next one, Bosch's hellish scenes of humans being devoured and tortured by creatures. Jeremy glanced over the paintings, and, without an ounce of discomfort or disgust, reached for the corner of one and moved it slightly up, aligning it now perfectly with the rest.

The elevator's door opened. He entered a room. In the distance were approximately 20 people, women and men, in business attire, sitting in modern silver-black, metallic chairs at a round table.

The table was massive, made of black glass, but positioned low, reaching their knees. The room had large windows, revealing the blue sky and clouds. Jeremy sat in the last remaining chair that was waiting for him.

"My legion, my wisest and most loyal ones," spoke the presiding woman who was sitting right across Jeremy. "The circle is now closed." She looked at Jeremy, "We can begin," she said and continued, "Pass me the effigy of human innocence and joy."

From his bag, Jeremy took out the teddy bear and slid it across the table to her. As her fingers touched it, transferring her coldness to it, the toy froze. She lifted it up and broke one of its paws. Keeping the paw in her hand, she passed the toy to the person next to her. That person broke a different body part, kept it, and passed the toy to the next person. All repeated this behavior until the final piece of the teddy bear reached the presiding woman.

"We are the pathways to darkness," she said. Everyone repeated after her.

"Do it, now," she commanded.

They all opened their palms, revealing the frozen pieces of the bear's body, which began to levitate above their opened hands. Suddenly, the pieces burst into flames and ashes fell into their palms. Everyone reached as far as they could towards the center of the table, leaving a trail of ash, beginning at the center, reaching back to where they were siting.

"Assume your positions," she said.

All present stepped onto the round table. Below them, in the depth of the table resembling a bottomless pit, 20 skulls, imprisoned in darkness, with gaping eye sockets and opened mouths, gazed up, as if terrified and begging for mercy from those who stood above them. The presiding woman stood on the table as well, and stepped to the middle of it. Below her, in the depth of the dark matter, was an image of the Earth, at the level of the skulls, rotating very slowly.

"Repeat after me," she commanded. Twenty voices, acting as her echoes, kept repeating her words: "We are the architects and rulers of the night, and we stand on the skulls of human plight. Our life is an eternal, powerful force that does not know hunger, as long as it is sheltered within a temple of freezing darkness. Its foundation is human suffering. The seven pillars are fear, poverty, hatred, disunity, sickness, murder and rage. The human race builds our temple. We supervise and help its work." She approached each one, landing her hand on their shoulders, as she continued:

"Repeat. We destroy countries, our own and foreign ones and bring them collapse, illness, torment, famine and poverty. We kill, pillage, steal, rape, take away huts and roofs over heads. We burn the innocent at the stakes, abuse and molest children, charge the poor for our services, and preach what we don't believe in. We make laws that foster crime, delay and disrupt justice. With money, we sustain all this evil and keep it repeating, day after day, century after century. We are everywhere, in the image of kings, queens, emperors and empresses, statesmen and politicians, chiefs of intelligence services and their agents, soldiers, priests and priestesses, attorneys, company CEOs and bankers.

At times we are ordinary citizens: fathers, mothers, spouses, and students that one hears about only when, in an instant, they take innocent lives, and clothe families in shock, shame, and despair. When we are among them, we grasp them firmly, wrapping around their souls and bodies like snakes, not releasing them from the grip of our bribery, threats, blackmail, and physical confrontation, demanding human darkness.

At times we do not intervene since there are humans who secure this darkness for us. We know no hunger in the temple of freezing darkness. We are the architects and the rulers of the night and stand on the skulls of human plight."

"Luckily for us, not everything is that dark," Jeremy spoke. "The human race, with its perpetuating horrors, has granted us a delicious, never-ending feast. I wonder why I haven't grown a big belly after millennia of being so well-fed?" Everyone laughed at his irony.

"Yes, Heremion," said the presiding woman. "But, something concerns me." Silence filled the room since she rarely showed concern. "Let's depart from the limitations of the human body and continue this conversation in conditions that yield a better reflection," she said, and added, "Legion, surrender to me your essence."

Suddenly, everyone lifted up from the surface of the table, as if gravity did not exist any longer. Hovering above the skulls, all turned heads towards the ceiling. With their mouths opened, they pronounced their names, with long exhalations. A wavy, dark smoke exited each mouth, moving toward the presiding woman, who breathed them all in with her nostrils. Then, she closed her eyes.

In another world, with three eclipsed suns in the red sky, in the middle of a frozen lake surrounded by snowy mountains, 19 plumes of smoke hovered above the icy surface, encircling a single, presiding smoke in the middle. The summit could continue.

"Humans will, sooner or later, realize, maybe in a thousand years, that they can be happy--and they will find a road to it. They discovered quantum physics, harnessed electricity, understood chemistry, invented computers and airplanes. It is just a matter of time until they will discover a path for overcoming crime, war, suffering. What will we do then? Die of starvation?" the presiding voice asked.

"With all due respect, Idolatra, I disagree," interrupted Jeremy. "All that they discovered and invented eventually leads to their suffering. From the discovery of quantum physics came the atomic bomb. With the advent of chemistry, drugs and poisons. Phones and computers are used to spy on and threaten and manipulate people. Television gives rise to propaganda, twisting and suppressing the truth. Airplanes and cars are used to murder. I can go on and on. But, as I have already said, we have been blessed with human darkness. They will never, I emphasize *never*, find peace and progress. We should be celebrating, not worrying. If we had human bodies right now, I would pour champagne in your glasses, and we would toast 'cheers' to each other." Everyone laughed.

Another male voice added, "Heremion is right. They will find neither peace nor happiness. The human race is a lost cause. The wheel of history will never cease to turn for them. No one will ever stop it. We are very fortunate for that state of affairs."

"True." A female voice added. "But, I hope the human race does not annihilate itself with its scientific 'progress'. I see a problem in *that*, actually. Not that they will become better, that certainly won't be the case, but that they will destroy themselves. What will happen to us then?"

"Exactly!" Another male voice chimed in. "Erfemina has a great point. Yet, the human race is tough, some will survive and repopulate the Earth. Even if they become extinct, wiped out from the face of the earth, we can employ genetics to clone them or modify apes, and derive humans from them. And the human beings will, sooner or later, repeat their past mistakes. No question about that. We'll help them with that, as we always have done."

"You are probably right, almost certainly," the voice of the presiding woman said. "But, let's suppose that you are wrong. Let's say that there is a leader in the future who will bring them progress. What then? If that happens, if there is no suffering any longer, no rage, no hatred, no racism, no wars, no crimes, we are the ones who will become extinct, not them. They will be the survivors then. Regardless of how impossible that scenario seems, what if that becomes reality? What if such a leader shows up? How do we prevent our extinction then?"

"We'll implement the protocol 14:26," a female voice responded. "It has always worked; it'll work again."

"Hear, hear!" All said in unison.

"So be it," Idolatra confirmed. "The meeting is over." She opened her eyes, standing in the middle of the round table, in human flesh, as dark smoke exited her mouth, spiraling out and entering the opened mouths of her levitating legion. Essences once again dispersed to their owners.

CHAPTER TWO

NISKALA

60 years later.

In his art studio, Nel worked tirelessly on his newest sculpture, The Wheel of History, without taking a break for hours. Niskala was sitting on a nearby couch, working on her laptop and admiring his work.

"History is a wheel that doesn't cease to turn," she commented, attempting to decipher the sculpture's meaning. "Wars, evil, suffering . . . everything repeats. Some good deeds too. But the bad side seems to repeat much more often. It dominates. A better future beckons us to its light, but our pasts imprison us in darkness, right? Am I interpreting your work correctly, love?"

"I wouldn't know how to say it any better, my dear. Yes, the wheel of history is relentless. Sad but so true," Nel responded, taking a sip of his drink.

"Yet, we can stop it. For good," she said, with a confident smile on her face.

"Oh, you want me to stop it? Just nod." Nel said, jokingly, holding a hammer in his hand, as if waiting for Niskala's permission to break the sculpture.

"Haha, you know very well what I meant. I intend to create a society where the Wheel does not exist."

"You and your noble dreams. That's why I adore you, Niskala! I wonder how you intend to do that. I believe in goodness and all, but it can't prevail. There will always be a struggle between good and evil. I'd say you're wasting your time with the project."

"I disagree. Humans have a potential, a hidden one. There is no fixed human nature. The negativity and darkness that we see in the world, it doesn't have to be like that. I'll buy a territory, a vast unpopulated land, from the government. There, children and new generations will be educated in the spirit of positive expectations."

"Positive expectations? About what exactly?" he asked.

"That everyone can be happy and that the road to that happiness consists of controlling negative emotions and nurturing positive moods by focusing on proper nutrition and sleep, physical exercise, meaningful romantic relationships, and strong parenting. Children will also learn that they will feel good when they help one another and when they reach a compromise. I can go on and on," she said with passion.

"All that sounds great, but when the children discover the Wheel of History, when they learn how destructive humans were in the past, all your lofty ideas will just become wishful thinking. The Wheel will grind your children, Niskala. Negative expectations will arise in them, and they will look back, into the past, into the image of who humans *were*, they will be terrified of that image, of others, and of themselves; they will be left without any faith in a better tomorrow."

"You are wrong, my dear," Niskala responded, coming closer to him, wrapping her arms around his neck. "I will be the one who stops the Wheel. Children will not even know about the bad side of human history. They will only know our good side and just a tiny bit of the bad one—just to caution them of the possibility of being destructive. They will expect goodness from people, and what they expect, that's what they'll give and get. The power of the mind to make ideas reality is nothing new to science."

"Ok, but what about the idea that we'll repeat our mistakes if we do not study history?" Nel asked.

"I couldn't disagree more. Our knowledge of history, turns the wheel of history," she said with firm conviction.

"I don't know, Niskala . . . that hiding of truth . . . people won't like that. I don't like it either, I must admit. It seems like you're wrong about this," Nel said.

"For the truth, Nel, we need to be ready . . . at some point my children will certainly learn about history, but not before they can fight off its dark side. The truth is sacred, and it neither should nor can remain hidden forever. I will only postpone it. When they are ready for it, the children will face it without being changed by it in any bad way. I'll turn a new page in human development. And if you want, you can be a part of it too."

"Of course, my love. I admire your enthusiasm to help humans become better. Perhaps it is best to jump into it and build that society to see if you are right or wrong. You may be right, after all." To Niskala's surprise, he swung the hammer and hit the sculpture, creating a crack from the bottom to the top. A large smile appeared on Niskala's surprised face. She knew that Nel rarely did anything impulsive, so she figured the crack was meant to improve the sculpture.

"Excellent!" Nel said, examining the crack and how it fit with the entire creation. "I think it turned out great. But, something is still missing—a tiny detail—an indication of freedom . . . a symbol of it—a departure from the Wheel—of transcendence."

"A bird, perhaps," Niskala suggested.

"You read my mind, love. A bird. That's it," he said, and quickly made a bird, painted it and placed it at the top of the wheel. Then he said, "Now, it's done. I'll call it 'Beyond the Wheel of

History.'" Niskala approached the Wheel, ran her hand over the surface, over the crack and patted the dove.

"I love it." She said. "It communicates everything we said so well. It's beautiful. So genuine. Mesmerizing," she said.

"I wonder," he persisted "what will happen when the government tries to take your money and get rid of you. Peace and prosperity are not what they are after. They benefit from wars, illness, disasters, terrorism. They'll oppose the idea of your society spreading throughout the world, and they'll see a plague in it. You'll, well, we will, attract a lot of powerful enemies—not only our government, but many other ones. Are you ready for that? They'll crucify us." Nel said.

"With every fiber of my being, I'm ready." Niskala said. "They'll try to destroy us, yes, but my team and I are anticipating it. We'll defend, successfully, what we believe is sacred." She said.

"How?"

"I'll show you once you move to the new society. As long as you are here, you are not safe. The less you know about our defense system, the better for all of us."

"Of course. When you secure the territory, I'll start packing." Nel said. "You and your team can count on me. I'd love to live in a better world. Or die trying to create it."

As Niskala had hoped, she purchased a fairly large, uninhabited territory from the government. The price included the land's statehood as well as its independence. The government embraced this unusual arrangement since it desperately needed money to pay off its debts, which had accumulated over decades of reckless wars, poor investments and borrowing, so it pulled strings to legitimize and finalize the process rather quickly. The sum was so immense that not only did the government pay off their entire debt, but they also ended up with a considerable surplus. For them, the government, it was all about the money that would ensure them a comfortable life and a status quo in domestic and foreign policy; however, for Niskala and her team, their money was just a valuable instrument to attain a much higher goal—to transcend the status quo and create a humanistic society instead.

Upon securing the territory, Niskala's plan was to address all citizens of the world proposing they become involved with her new society. Before spending more money on purchasing air time on TV stations, however, she wanted to try posting a video on the internet. She hoped it would be seen by many people and that her team would not even need to spend additional money on air time. Financing was not an issue at all, but her collaborators, including herself, firmly believed in wise spending, pouring money into the genesis of this new society, instead of giving more money outside of it, promoting a dysfunctional civilization.

Niskala was their elected leader and spokesperson. Her charisma made her an excellent choice for connecting with a wide audience. Her team created the video in which she first introduced herself as well as all the members of her team—known and unknown physicists, chemists, athletes, biologists, attorneys, physicians, economists, business people, artists, one of whom was Nel, philosophers, and people from various other domains of life. What they all had in common was that they were all wealthy (decreasing the chance of being corrupted by money). These were all very successful people in their chosen professions, and each had at least a university degree. It was also very important that these people were not associated with any scandals.

In the video, Niskala invited people from around the world to relocate to her society, a beautifully natural environment that had just started the process of building roads, houses, schools, hospitals, and all other aspects of the new society. In the video, she said that this new society, Solaris, would be based on new principles: the lowest bills (electricity, water, gas, internet, association fees, etc.) in the world; the lowest cost of medical insurance and education in the world; the lowest taxes in the world. Everyone who would enroll at the new society's university with a plan to obtain a degree, and those who already held a degree, would be given a free apartment for life. They would enjoy a place spacious enough for that person (if he or she had no family) or an apartment suitable for the size of that person's family. Every apartment would be fully furnished with new furniture and appliances, with a garage and two new cars. The person would be guaranteed employment, within his/her chosen field, immediately after the degree was obtained. In the video, Niskala walked through several actual apartments, highlighting different floor plans, showing off their modern, bright, and stunning architecture, which was in the shape of a dome. In Niskala's society, a dome was a building code motif due to its various advantages over the traditionally shaped buildings.

Then, she was featured driving one of the new cars through gorgeous, newly built neighborhoods with lush vegetation, swimming pools and jacuzzis, explaining that this would be a society with no bad neighborhoods and that all that was shown in the video would be the standard for everyone. So, Niskala asked rhetorically why would someone even want to engage in crime when Solaris would already provide a very comfortable existence. "Exactly," she answered her own question.

Niskala *could* argue that other societies did not care about their citizens enough, that many citizens became criminals due to societies' failure to provide opportunities and a more comfortable life, that those societies did not do enough to prevent the genesis of crime. She could say that only after crime happened, only then, and too late, governments spent a significant amount of money on the prison system, attempting to reform criminals. She could criticize that pattern characteristic of other societies, the practice of not investing in the *prevention* of crime, but she didn't. She was different, oriented towards constructive thinking. Her philosophy was to embrace a positive perspective, without letting negative thoughts and feelings enter her mind. So, she voiced no criticism, no mudding of others; she talked only about the good life in her society.

Niskala said that people who would come to live in Solaris would need to commit to doing something in return for all that would be provided for their well-being. People would need to forget about the bad parts of human history; to let go and to raise children, as much as they could, without reference to any aggression, wars, crime, prejudice, discrimination, or similar negative human behaviors that had plagued civilization in the past. Her team's ideas were to expose people, especially children, to a positive environment so that their expectations of fellow-humans would bring about their own virtuous behavior. Movies, music videos, art, and literature would be edited so that the negative aspects would not be shown to children nor to adults.

The truth about human decadence from the past, she explained, would not need to be hidden forever; it would be merely delayed for a time, until it couldn't contaminate or negatively shape human behavior any longer. The way people learn, she said, is through observation and imitation; thus, her new society would provide role models displaying cooperation, respect, compassion, help, compromise, peaceful resolution, and other positive behaviors. These patterns would be rewarded in this new society, since when behaviors are rewarded, they tend to repeat.

Niskala also said that all decisions that her team made in the past, and those that it would make in the future, would be based on voting, on the will of the majority. After they would come up with a certain law, the citizens of the society would be able to vote on it, and the will of the majority would be the final decision that would be implemented. She also stated that a good portion of her team's money would be allocated to tapping into an energy source in the universe that would be accessible for everyone, for free, so that electricity and other utility bills would not exist any longer. Since harnessing this source of energy was only likely, she warned that it may not be attainable in reality, but that her society would at least contribute brilliant scientists in an attempt to secure it. So, she did not make unrealistic promises, as politicians often do; instead, as she addressed people, they could sense that she was a genuine person, with hope and vision, but with a trace of healthy skepticism, caution, and awareness of limitations. She added that even though she could not promise anything, her team firmly believed, and sincerely hoped, that the discovery would be made due to this new, humanistic environment that would inspire the human mind for yet unseen breakthroughs.

A considerable amount of money, she added, would be invested towards discoveries of cures for various illnesses. The human intellect would, no doubt, flourish as never before in this new environment, and it would not be long until amazing discoveries and inventions would be made in medicine, as well as in other fields. Perhaps, she said, her society would be able to slow down, or even stop the aging process altogether, via likely breakthroughs in genetics. But, she emphasized that all these predictions were not promises; these were just likely, yet uncertain, developments in the positive environment her team was building.

When the video was released, Niskala's team had no idea how people would respond to it. The video was professionally created with cutting-edge equipment and cinematography, and Niskala charismatically delivered a powerful message, emphasizing that each person from her group was accomplished, educated, and acted with moral integrity. But, regardless of all those positive aspects of the video, even to the members of her group, the video sounded too-good-to-be-true, like some fairy-tale. So, they didn't know whether the video would resonate with the people or whether they would dismiss it. Still, the team could only hope that the video would, at least, make people cautiously curious and inspire them to join Solaris on a trial basis.

A day or so after the video was released, it went "viral." In just a couple of days it became a phenomenon that everyone was talking about. In fact, it became the most watched video in history within days. Major TV stations did not cover it at all; they completely ignored it since they were more focused on negative news, but Niskala and her team had a different philosophy about what interested people and what should interest them, so through the power of the internet, Niskala's video made a serious impact on people. The number of viewers was growing rapidly, and it was amazing to watch this development.

Underneath the video, in the comments section, the vast majority of comments were positive, with a few negative ones here and there, but nobody responded to those. Nobody! Obviously, people were hungry for something new, for Niskala's orientation that ignored negativity and focused on the positive instead. Not surprisingly, the negative comments, after a few days, ceased completely. When those individuals were not rewarded with attention from others, they did not continue posting their negative views. In fact, Niskala's team, with sophisticated software, detected that the vast majority of the people who were initially posting negative comments had changed their names and started posting positive comments instead. They changed their perspective, which again indicated the power of positive information to change the way one thinks. But, what did all this mean? Was Niskala's team successful only in the virtual reality of the internet? Would anyone actually come to Niskala's society? The answer was yes, millions!

Over the next several months, numerous people, around three million, from all over the world, flocked to Solaris. Some of them were the unemployed who had nothing to lose; some were refugees displaced from their homes due to wars; some felt a need for a change in their lives, to turn away from human failures and embrace a more promising future; some were adventurers, enticed by something new, different and seemingly positive. When anyone who was processed at the entrance into Solaris was asked why they chose to relocate, the vast majority explained that they were overwhelmed, bombarded with negative news and events in the outside world, that all that negativity affected their moods and their lives, and that Solaris seemed to be a place to rest, a sanctuary from all that burden, a place where one could enjoy a more positive life. Also, almost everyone stated that they loved Niskala, that they connected with her on a deep level and saw her as the personification of hope, honesty, and love. The vast majority of the people said that they wanted a leader just like her.

Although a lot of people came to Niskala's society from all over the world, Solaris did not stop people from immigrating. Because of this choice, many governments were very concerned, about a significant loss of employees and tax-payers. There were now many available jobs, and it was predicted that the people who were waiting for work would simply replace the ones who left, but that was not the case—those who were unemployed left as well.

An urgent meeting of the world-wide governments was summoned, aimed at deciding what to do about this situation. Arguments were made that Niskala's society was a threat to the economy of all countries, that a possibility of free energy might destroy many industries throughout the world since all those industries depended on paying customers. What if cars started running on the free energy that Niskala spoke of? Would that destroy companies that depended on customers buying their gasoline for cars? And what would happen to the electric companies? Would they go out of business too? What about their employees? How would these businesses and their employees pay taxes then? Also, the potential discoveries of cures for illnesses seemed unhealthy for the economy as well. What would physicians do who specialized in treating illnesses that no longer existed? What would rehabilitation specialists do? What would become of the fields of transplantation and prosthetics, or of the field of nursing? If they all lost their jobs, countless tax-payers would be lost as well. When, people do not need medications any longer, what would the pharmaceutical companies do, what would the pharmacists do? And how would all these companies and employees pay taxes if they were out of business? So, curing people became a huge problem in the minds of government representatives.

Governments came up with a unanimous decision—to launch a military operation, called "The Exorcist," aimed at eliminating Niskala and her group. In their eyes, Niskala and her team were destabilizing the structure of the world, and the world would be much better off without such misled efforts. In their opinion, Niskala was a subversive, regressive element that was determined not to save the world but to destroy it. In the best-case scenario, according to some governments, she was a naive utopian, a romantic idealist, an infantile dreamer whose society would sooner rather than later collapse, and that, in the end, the ones who would suffer the most would be the millions of tricked people, who would lose everything, including hope. They would get sicker and poorer than ever before, lose their humanity and sanity. They would become wild beasts, impulsive savages, who would devour one another. What would happen, the question was raised, when these barbarians of Solaris attack the rest of the civilized world?

Some governments argued that Niskala was an extremely dangerous, delusional cult-leader, who would soon isolate her society, close its borders, put people in uniforms, shave their heads, change their names, make them blindly repeat meaningless sentences, and completely brainwash them. The time was coming, those experts prophesized, when she would command her followers to terrorize the rest of the world, and after the ensuing blood-bath require her blind followers to commit mass-suicide. It happened in the past, they said, and it would happen again with Niskala. History repeats itself, they argued.

They all, however, were unable to see, or better, did not *want* to see, that Niskala was just the opposite of all of their negative portrayals. She was all about freedom, allowing people to come and go as they pleased. She was about nurturing individuality and uniqueness, personal growth, cooperation, peace, democracy, equality and diversity. She nurtured critical thinking based on asking cogent questions, challenging leaders' views, analyzing arguments, being skeptical, gathering facts, moving beyond superstition and speculation. Governments did not want to see that cooperation with Niskala and her brilliant group of people might solve the world's problems and ensure progress and stability. They did not want to see Niskala's society become an example for the rest of the world to follow. Different governments had different perceptions of what was wrong with Niskala, her team and society, but they all agreed on the necessity of "The Exorcist."

Generals of various governments met. They suspected that Niskala's team was not foolish, far from it, considering how many brilliant minds were associated with her, and that they must have anticipated this kind of reaction from governments. They suspected, therefore, that Niskala had a military response prepared. They did not know what kind of defense since all their efforts at satellite surveillance had failed, probably due to Niskala's sophisticated anti-spying technology. The generals thought that in this particular situation, dealing with such an opponent, a significant amount of the military force would be required to successfully implement "The Exorcist." Regardless of the weapons she had, they decided they should throw every kind of destructive force in their arsenal at her, the "pandemonium" as they called it. It would ensure a swift and effective massive strike that would eliminate Niskala and her society, so that in a few days they could put all that behind and continue with their busy lives.

Also, the generals thought that the display of their full military capacity would be a good demonstration of power with all the world watching, in case some other lunatic in the future, similar to Niskala, dared to come up with messianic delusions of grandeur. It would be best, the generals agreed, to make a real spectacle of all this and involve TV stations, like a popular reality show, unscripted, with real blood, like the Roman Coliseum gladiator fights. In this way, they reasoned, people could have exceptional entertainment, but at the same time, be reminded of who the bosses were, the best gladiators, the champions of the world, men and women in uniform not to be messed with, especially when they united and played on the same dream team.

Before the unleashing of The Exorcist, the governments wanted to get into Niskala's head. They wanted to induce fear in her, concern and pain, to distract her with those feelings, to destabilize her so that she would not function optimally during their operation. So, they kidnapped Nel. He was making last minute preparations to relocate to her society, but this never happened. He just disappeared. The kidnappers did not want to make a trade with Niskala, to ask her for something in return for him since they knew she would not negotiate with them, that she was determined to defend her "humanistic society" no matter how much she or her loved ones were hurting. There was no information about what happened to him, where he was held, or whether he was tortured or killed; she only received his harmonica. He liked to play it, and was never without it, carrying it in his pocket always: it was a precious gift from Niskala. That was the only thing left from him. She was devastated, of course, but she found strength to put her despair about Nel aside, and concentrate on the larger purpose in her life: promoting humanity.

...

Dawn had just broken. A vast military force, joined with TV reporters, was approaching Niskala's society. There were countless trucks, tanks, drones and helicopters. Trucks moved along the road, tanks covered the vast fields, helicopters and drones hovered above like giant mosquitos. The loud buzzing and relentless pandemonium made the earth shake. Niskala was prepared. She waited for them in the middle of the road. Behind her, the road between two adjacent mountains led to Solaris. She was sitting at a coffee table, sipping her morning cup, waiting for the army to come closer. It appeared she was alone, but two mighty allies accompanied her--one was nature, the other technology. She took another sip of coffee. The army was getting closer, but still in the distance, she could not see them with her naked eyes, only on her phone's radar. In a few minutes they would be close enough for the projectiles and snipers to try to take her out.

"Ten minutes to being in the opponent's range," the voice warned from her device.

She touched the button on her phone. The signal went underground to four towers with a dome on top of each, equally spaced along the border of Solaris. Instantaneously and in a synchronized manner, they began emerging from below the Earth's surface, each sending a beam of solid white energy to the cloudless, blue sky. Clouds rapidly formed producing a sphere-like entanglement of lightning bolts that forcefully collapsed onto the domes charging the towers. In a few seconds after the impact, one of the towers emitted a laser beam, connecting all four of them. The beam widened vertically into an energy shield that separated Niskala and the army yet to appear. The barrier resembled an illuminated, thin sheet of green fog, rising from the ground towards the sky, then curving above Solaris like a protective dome.

Through binoculars, she could now see the approaching army, and at that same moment, when the opponents could also see her, snipers fired at her. But the bullets hit the green fog barrier in front of her and just disappeared. More ammunition was fired at her from several helicopters, yet the shield absorbed it all. Shocked and confused, the army halted its attack. Trucks and tanks stopped, and the helicopters landed, until a solution could be found. TV stations and reporters were immediately ordered to stop transmitting the live feed, since this was now portraying Niskala successfully defending herself, and the situation did not favor the army at all: they were embarrassed. Thus, governments acted fast, secretly unleashing a prepared terrorist attack somewhere else, diverting attention from the blunder with Niskala. The focus would now be on successfully fighting a terrorist crisis instead. But, Niskala's team was anticipating this development, and they used the internet for a free, live feed of the actual situation that was unfolding.

Niskala touched the screen on her phone. Instantly a wave of green energy detached from the shield, and like a supernova explosion, enveloped the army. When the wave went through a soldier or a TV reporter, that person's visual field became white with nothing in it other than the infinite whiteness. Then, in a couple of seconds, that whiteness transitioned into a scene very different from the road, field and the mountains ahead of them. Each soldier saw a scene with something beautifully touching, blissful, something sublime that made him or her feel happy. Smiles graced their faces and tears of happiness poured down their cheeks. What all of them saw was incredibly real. One soldier saw the birth of his child; someone else witnessed her dead child resurrected and well again; another person laid eyes on a deceased friend alive again; another person was on a dream date; someone else, taking the form of a child, was fishing with his father; someone else was kissed by her husband, while another person was transported to childhood, being hugged and kissed by her mother. They all felt transported to a very different reality, as if had gone through some portal, connecting them with different time or space.

The experience was so real, so all encompassing, so overwhelming, that it was impossible to separate from the grasp of that wonderful hallucination. It didn't feel at all like something dream-like, or a fabrication of their minds; it felt as if it was really happening, all with scents, visual information, sounds, tastes, and all other sensory aspects of an actual situation. In essence, all that was the fabrication of their minds, of their brains being stimulated by the energy of the wave. Niskala touched another button, and the wave stopped disseminating the information, and everyone's positive experience ended abruptly. The mountains, the road, the field, and Niskala at the table were in front of them again.

Everyone exposed to the wave was suddenly confused, disoriented, lost, and desperate for not being able to hold onto that amazingly powerful, unbelievably real happiness that was so abruptly taken away. Suddenly, everyone felt profoundly detached from the present reality of attacking Niskala; they felt this was so trivial, it muddied the sacred bliss inside of themselves. They felt they were wasting their precious time on earth on doing something so wrong, instead of pursuing what made them happy, or being with people whom they loved, or being in places and situations that promoted happiness. The next wave carried Niskala's voice in it, but it was no ordinary voice. They felt that her voice was somehow attached to them, to their clothes, jumping from one arm to the other, from leg to leg, from shirt to face. The voice felt alive, like a living presence.

She said, "I release you. You are free to go. You have a choice. You can go back to your lives or you can choose to stay with me. Together, we can build a better world. If you want to leave, nobody is stopping you. Just go." She paused, then continued, "I showed you how true happiness feels. But, if you continue to attack me, you will be attacking humanity itself, and the next wave that you feel will make you experience your worst fears. This is my final warning and the moment of your decision. Are you staying with me to build peace, or are you leaving in peace?" She asked.

Nobody moved for a few seconds. Then, something extraordinary happened. The doors of trucks, helicopters, and tanks opened, and many soldiers and reporters left vehicles, weapons and cameras behind and walked, with peaceful intentions, towards

Niskala. In that wave of bliss, they had encountered an extraordinary technology, something revolutionary, and they viewed Niskala as someone who was not of their time, someone decades ahead, somebody deserving a chance to cultivate a better human society, somebody they wanted to help. If they believed in miracles and wizards, this would be proof of that, but since they believed in science, the happiness they experienced was the evidence of a highly advanced one. In just a few seconds Niskala had shown them the purpose of their existence—to be happy, and they felt that through Niskala and her vision, they could rediscover that ultimate feeling above all feelings, and make it last.

Niskala proved their superiors very wrong—she was not the personification of evil, as some had said she was. If she had been, she would not have let them go. If she were who they claimed she was, she would destroy them, pulverize them with her weapons, or capture them and ask their governments for something in return. She was not a delusional dreamer either, as she was portrayed to be, since her advanced machines worked more effectively than any weapon they had known. Her approach to fighting was very different and more advanced than anything they had encountered, heard, or read about elsewhere; she gave them something extraordinarily positive at first, something to treasure for the rest of their lives, and when she withdrew that from them, the removal of that all-encompassing bliss was absolutely devastating. So, she fought in a unique way, without really fighting. She won by opening their hearts to what is really important in life—the fulfillment of happiness.

The soldiers were deeply moved when they saw that she was one who stood against so many, that she was what their superior officers always said that a soldier should be—an army of one. She was exactly that. Without fear, a personification of bravery, she had calmly defended something she had believed in. People. An idea. Humanity. And she showed mercy in granting freedom to those who came to murder her, who had taken her lover from her. They surrendered to her out of a deep sense of respect and admiration, and wanted to be led by her. There were a few soldiers who were skeptical, and they turned around and left. They didn't stay long, however; they came back with their families over the next few days and joined Niskala's world, supporting her mission.

Those who were issuing commands, miles and miles away, in their cozy offices and comfortable situation rooms, far away from the battlefield, as usual, sending others to fight their wars, were not missed or cared about any longer. Niskala opened the soldiers' eyes. The soldiers realized that without them, their superiors were, simply put, nothing. Presidents, generals, kings, emperors, without their obedient soldiers, were just empty titles, just words. Without soldiers, those in command were completely unimportant, insignificant, ineffective, and weak. Niskala did not even need to release a wave of fear on them; the chain of command fractured, the creators of the chess game lost their pawns--that was already their worst nightmare.

The generals and world leaders saw the possibility of multitudes of industries collapsing, millions upon millions of soldiers abandoning military forces, and they immediately understood that Niskala's mind-altering weapons were far superior than any others on the planet. They were frightened by these immense powers Niskala displayed and realized they had no idea what other extraordinary technology and mind-altering powers she had hidden in her arsenal. It was not long before the leaders of the world asked Niskala for reconciliation and for her guidance. They accepted that they could not defeat her, so they decided to join her, instead. Ironically, those who only recently most passionately advocated her murder, were now endorsing her on the TV left and right. She despised that political circus, but she tolerated it for the sake of possible peace and a real change in the world. She did not trust the world leaders at all, she knew that they were fickle politicians that turned only in the direction of their self-serving interests, but she worked with them, cautiously. She proposed a solution, one in which she and her team would lead the planet, while the rest of the governments would be their administration, and implement their philosophy. In turn, her team would make sure that there was a very smooth transition, with no collapsed economy, into a world that reflected the principles of Solaris.

The leaders of the world accepted this arrangement since they feared Niskala and her group. They realized that she would be relentless in the pursuit of her ideals, and they expected another demonstration of her technological supremacy if they did not obey. Secretly, they talked amongst themselves, saying that Niskala appeared to be so nice, so polite, so forgiving, so warm, but that all that simply must be a mask, a pretense, a charade, hiding a ferocious beast under all that superficial beauty and charm. They did not realize that there was no monster inside her, that they did not know her at all, that they were misperceiving her. The beast that they were imagining, actually, was a monster lurking within themselves.

At an international conference, a general asked Niskala very directly: "Many of us wondered, Niskala, did you use Tesla's technology when you defended Solaris? It seemed to us that you did because the shapes of your towers were almost identical to his."

"Yes, I did," she revealed. "My team was guided by Tesla in constructing the defense system."

"You mean you obtained Tesla's *writings* and/or *drawings*? He died in the 1943," another general inquired.

"No, we were guided by Tesla himself." Confusion covered their faces. She added, "We contacted him; some would call it his 'soul,' by using the recording of his life energy."

"I don't believe we understand, Niskala," the general looked around. "A recording of his life energy?"

"Have you or anyone else in the room ever heard of a video or voice recording of Nikola Tesla?" she asked. Everyone was quiet.

"No." The general answered.

"We are not aware of anyone possessing those items," another general responded.

"Well, I do. Those items have been hidden, given only to those who genuinely want to build a better human society, who would die for it. So, I had the privilege of receiving them. The video featuring Tesla and his recorded voice contain his unique energy signature that can be matched with the one in the universe, locating his entity, soul, consciousness, or whatever we want to call someone's passed away personality. We contacted him that way, and he was willing to help."

"I'm sure we are all curious to know who kept those items hidden for years. Some secret society, perhaps? Give us a hint, at least."

"No, it was Tesla himself." Everyone was confused in the room. "I received the items from him personally. He can materialize himself anywhere, anytime."

"The items, the voice and video, can you show them to us? We would very much like to see that rarity."

"Are *you* willing to die for humanity?" she asked.

"Niskala, I know that our armies fought you; it was a time of animosity between us, but that was our version of humanity, so, yes, we are willing to die for humanity."

"Well, Tesla has a different vision of humanity, a vision that matches mine. In addition, generals, those who fought me were your *soldiers*. I don't recall seeing any of *you* on the battlefield."

Thus, a new era began. The golden age of human civilization with Niskala presiding as the leader of the unified world. She was admired by people throughout the planet proud to have, finally, such an incredible leader who worked tirelessly against the status quo, who put humankind on track to true progress. She was a leader beyond the wheel of history.

...

Long before she became the leader of the world, Niskala learned that for great deeds one needs to have a sharp, calm mind, and in order to possess these qualities, one needs a healthy body; thus, she engaged in physical exercise almost daily. One seemingly ordinary morning she took her usual route, briskly walking up her favorite hill, one from which she could see a portion of Solaris and the mountains that sheltered it. When she reached the top of the hill, however, something unusual happened—a dense fog appeared. It was so surprisingly thick that she could not see anything in front of her, not even her outstretched arm. She only heard the sound of some type of a gate or a door opening… and a baby's cry coming from that direction. There was something hidden in that fog, an object of some sort and a child, and it seemed that it opened for her, awaiting her... But, making a step in any direction, surrounded with such fog, was dangerous and potentially deadly (she could fall off a cliff); so, she sat on the ground, without moving and closed her eyes. She calmed her mind completely, got in touch with her consciousness and released it, let it detach from her body. She visualized a glowing, thread-like umbilical cord connecting herself with her ascended soul, and like a kite in the wind, she could now see everything down below, the fog, the contours of her body briefly becoming visible, and a glimpse of some large, round object protruding from the fog. Niskala's tethered soul was a set of eyes leading her through the fog, instructing her to make several steps in one direction, then to make a turn and a few additional steps in a particular direction before she finally reached the object. She touched its surface. It was made of stone. The fog became a bit thinner. On that stone were skulls, and she recognized the object—it was a huge wheel of history, almost identical to the one that Nel had made in his studio. The object was adorned with skulls, as well as bas-reliefs of battles, but it lacked the crack running from the bottom to the top, as well as the bird Nel placed on top. High above, there was an opening in the wheel from which the cry of a baby was coming. The only thing Niskala could do was to climb up, using the skulls like steps. She reached the opening and entered a hallway, also made of stone. There were torches on the walls leading to the chamber with a cradle holding a baby.

But, before revealing what happened next, it must be said that there are different accounts of how Niskala reached the chamber. According to some storytellers, Niskala did not use her astral projection or out-of-body experience, but sitting on the ground, embraced by the fog, she pulled out her necklace, and from it she took a small, thin, long object, like a whistle, and blew into it. The object did not produce any sound, at least not one perceived by humans, and she put it in her lap, closed her eyes patiently and waited. In a few minutes a bat, an albino one, flew to her, hovering in front of her face. Niskala did not say anything to it; she just intended for the bat to fly into the fog and guide her to the object. The bat sensed her will and did exactly that, using its clicking sounds to locate the object, and she followed it straight to the wheel. But, there is another account about how she found her way in the fog—she closed her eyes and used her tongue to produce her own clicking technique, which bounced off the objects, creating faint yet sufficient contours in her mind. Only a handful of people in the world have ever been able to master this technique. So, she vaguely saw a tree, a bush, then the wheel, and she walked to it.

Within the wheel, in the chamber with the baby, torches were burning on the walls. There was an opening in the ceiling, right above the cradle, and a beam of natural light fell upon the baby, illuminating it. Niskala saw a large, black snake descending vertically on the wall, moving slowly in the direction of the cradle. She quickly took several torches, placing them around the cradle, so the snake could not approach. Leaning over the cradle, Niskala smiled at the baby and gently caressed its head. Poor baby, it was cold, naked and not covered with anything, yet it immediately stopped crying when it saw Niskala's smiling face. The child touched her nose and cheeks, looked her straight in the eyes and smiled back. That was enough for Niskala to instantly fall in love with the innocent, lonely and unprotected child. She quickly took off her jacket, wrapped the baby in it, and took it in her arms. Was the baby abandoned? Whose baby was it? Where did its parents go? Was it imprisoned by the wheel? Many questions were going through her mind until a crow flew into the room. It held something in its beak. It was a ring—a large, round one with many tiny prisms on its surface. The crow flew into the beam of light, hovering above the cradle, and as the beam touched the prisms, a rainbow-like reflection appeared on the wall. Niskala came closer. It was a document, stating that Niskala had adopted the baby on that same day. Niskala saw that the document was valid; it had the seal and all the signatures and official authentication that made it legally binding. The only things missing were her signature and the baby's name. She felt that if she took the ring, her signature would appear in the document on the wall. So, she took it from the crow's beak and placed it on her finger bathed in the light. Immediately, on the wall, in the rainbow image of the document, her signature appeared. That's how the baby became hers. Right there she gave the baby the name *Nora*, which means light. Niskala moved her hand back into the beam, and on the wall, in the document, the baby's name was written.

Niskala knew that the child was not a peace offering by whoever placed the wheel there. It was also not meant to be her reward for creating a humanistic world, and it certainly wasn't anyone's friendly gesture either. The baby was a tactic of war. Niskala's opponent, whoever it was, was trying to make her vulnerable. Now, having a child, being emotionally attached to it, would make Niskala easier to manipulate and harm. That was the only reason that the baby was there. Like the story of the Trojan Horse, Nora was a gift, containing potential destruction for Niskala. It was a sinister move from those who turn the wheel of history. Niskala recognized that she was becoming more vulnerable than ever, but regardless of that feeling, she held the baby tightly, kissed its head, and left the wheel with the child in her arms, knowing that during difficult times, it would be her love towards Nora that would give her strength to prevail.

CHAPTER THREE

NEL'S TEAR

Several years later.

A bird flew easily and playfully across a long, green field, soon reaching a castle in the shape of a female hand. The thumb was touching the index finger, and the rest of the fingers were slightly bent facing the sun. Between the thumb and the index finger was a sunflower petal, as if the hand was about to return a petal lost by the sun. Each finger had painted nails with stained glass windows of cobalt blue and red.

The bird landed on a ledge of an arched window, staring motionlessly into the world on the other side of the glass. Then it knocked on the glass with its beak. The long, tapered fingers of Niskala's hand gently touched the handle from the other side and turned it. Both halves of the window slowly opened, like the gate of a sanctuary in front of a traveler desiring rest. In her gently scented palm were granules of bird-food, scattered over the landscape of her life. The hungry beak approached and tickled her hills, valleys and rivers.

A colorful group of children was already in front of the castle.

"My Majesty, when you will join us?" a black boy asked.

"Children, I am not a majesty. Just call me Niskala." She disagreed with the lifestyle and mindset of those "majesties" pampered in opulence while their people were stricken by poverty, "majesties" who were often deluded that they were worthier than the ordinary people. "I am coming. I'm almost done getting ready," Niskala said.

"But, your Majesty," a girl said, cuddling with a sunflower, "you are already soooo perfect." She raised the flower towards Niskala's window.

"We beg you to hurry," someone yelled.

"I'll wait for you even until... until dark, your Majesty. And after dark, if I have to," a chubby boy said, his head lifted dreamily to the sky.

"I'm coming, I'm coming," she said and closed the window. She appeared at the entrance of her castle in a long, white robe. She threw off the sandals from her feet and joyfully stepped into a limitless grass field with yellow flowers and blue sky above.

"Niskala! Niskala!" Children ran towards her. She kneeled and spread her arms as if she could hug them all at once. They hugged and kissed her, and the children behind her covered her eyes with their palms so that she had to guess who they were. She held several hands at once, and the smallest children climbed on her back and, like little monkeys, hung around her neck. She was so delighted to see children of various skin colors, ethnic groups, and cultures, enjoying the innocence of their childhood, in the same place and together.

"Niskala, Niskala!" they giggled until their stomachs began hurting with joy. Then, when everyone was properly exhausted, Niskala sat on the grass, and everyone did the same. She lay on her back and put her arms behind her head. And everyone did the same. Together they looked into the sky, as if they were waiting for something to happen. Several birds appeared.

"Where do birds have their houses? Is it in the sky?" someone asked.

"Every bird has its house on the earth," Niskala said.

"But why not in the sky, when it's so big?"

"And beautiful."

"And blue."

"The clouds have their homes in the sky, why don't birds?"

"And the sun and stars. They all live in the sky."

"And the moon."

"Yes," Niskala said, "but birds only fly there. Their houses can't be in the sky because they cannot fly endlessly. The sky doesn't have trees, or branches, or nests, like the earth does. Imagine that suddenly a strong wind picked up, or thunder began. What would happen to bird houses in the sky then? They would be blown away like a feather." And she blew into a nearby dandelion, scattering its crown.

"But what about the clouds?"

"And the sun and stars?"

"And the moon?"

"Birds are different," Niskala continued. "They fly in the sky, but their houses are here on earth. They are born here with their brothers and sisters. Here, they see their parents for the first time; here their parents feed them and take care of them; here their wings and bodies become strong. From their homes they fly to the sky. And later, after their marvelous adventures in the sky, they always come back to their homes on earth to gather strength for their next flight. And all those other things, like the moon, the sun and the clouds, they are all born in the sky. They always stay there, and they never land on earth. Those are the inhabitants of the sky, you're right. But what are we going to do now? We haven't even started yet." Niskala pointed to the flock that was flying above her castle.

"To start what, Niskala? Tell us," someone said.

"What, what? Tell us, tell us." Everyone was curious.

Niskala turned her head slightly, covering her eyes from the Sun with her arm. "Well, that is part of my surprise for you," she said.

"Surprise? You have a surprise for us?"

"What kind of a surprise? Tell us, tell us."

"Actually," Niskala continued, "I have several surprises for you all."

"Show us, show us. Now, now."

"Ok, but first everyone will have to do something for me."

"What? What? We'll do it."

"Everyone will have to dig a hole," Niskala explained.

"Really? That's easy! Let's dig. Hurry!" the children yelled, jumping and running around Niskala.

She stood up and walked towards the side wall of her castle, where a cover concealed a pile of something. She pulled it aside, exposing wooden poles, shovels, plastic buckets, a yellow cement-mixer, cement and lime. She put some lime in a bucket, then, poured the lime on the grass in front of the children, drawing a circle.

"And now," she said, "each of you take some lime with a can... go and get it from there... and then draw a circle like I did." The children ran towards the pile with tools, and did as Niskala directed.

"Excellent! Now, take a shovel. One of you will hold the shovel, just like this, and two others will stand on each side of the shovel. Come closer; let's demonstrate. You come here, you here, good. I'm holding the shovel. And... see, the shovel just slides into the ground under my weight. Do this several times, and it will be easy to take out the dirt and to dig a hole. Everyone will have a hole, and don't forget to help each other." The children diligently began working on their holes.

"Now, let's fill the buckets with cement. Who wants to mix the cement with me? Well, I can't use you all. Ok, I'll close my eyes, and I'll point to someone. Ok, you, and... you." She opened her eyes and called those children to go with her.

"We'll take care of this quickly," she said, and the cement was mixed in no time. While some children helped to pour the cement into the buckets, other children were bringing empty buckets and taking filled buckets to their holes.

"Put the buckets into the holes. Watch me. Just like this. Done! And now, when everything is ready, everyone will take a pole and stick it into the cement. Support the pole for a few minutes, like this, so it stays straight while the cement hardens. Excellent! You are doing a great job. You must be some special children, as you learn so quickly, huh? Now, slowly put the dirt and the grass you dug up over the buckets that are in the holes you made." Many wooden poles were sticking out from the grass.

"When are we going to see our surprise, Niskala?"

"Yes, when?"

"I'll show you only one now, and later I'll show you more. Come with me; you are my guests now." She opened the door to her castle.

"Let's go, let's go. Let's see Niskala's home." The children were euphoric. One by one they entered Niskala's home.

The entrance hallway led into a spacious garden. The light coming from the stained-glass windows illuminated the most unusual orchids, ferns and trees. A large chameleon was on a tree branch, attracting the children with its statue-like position and its funny, ever-circling eyes, which revealed his confusion with so many visitors. In the center of the grass-covered room was a small stream, meandering toward a lake outside the castle.

"Swans! Look, swans!" the children cried in unison as a group of white and black swans approached the glass wall from outside of the castle. Their graceful motions were reflected in the calm water covered with water lilies. Niskala pressed a button, lifting the glass wall, and the swans quietly floated towards the children lining the side of the pool. Other swans began coming in, each pushing a floating ring with its beak. Each ring carried a present wrapped in shiny paper with a bow on the top.

"Wow! Look, look..."

"Here you are. Each of you can take your surprise, and let's open them outside, on the grass. Wait for me, and we will open them together," Niskala instructed, sitting on the edge of the pool, and petting a swan.

When the children took their presents, they said goodbye to the birds and left the castle. When the last swan swam away, Niskala lowered the glass wall and joined the children outside. The children were very impatient as they tried to imagine what could possibly be inside the boxes. They shook them, they held them to their ears for a clue, they inspected each other's presents, but they couldn't guess what treasures were inside.

"Go ahead, open them now." A myriad of excited hands began opening the presents. In the ocean of double-sided tape, torn paper, ribbon and flying confetti, they discovered the secret of their surprise. Everyone had been given a wooden birdhouse, each one unique. Some were round, while some were shaped like diamonds; others looked like stars and half-moons; there were also some that resembled Saturn, pyramids, towers and many other shapes. Each present was a real little house with a door, windows and a roof. The children loved them.

"Aren't they wonderful?" Niskala said. "Each birdhouse has space for bird food. We'll take care of the bird food later, but now I would like one surprise from everyone of you." The children wondered why she wanted to be surprised. What would she like? How could they possibly surprise Niskala?

"I would like very much," Niskala said, "for you to paint the birdhouses any way you want. There," she pointed to another pile next to the castle. "You will find paints, brushes, crayons and all the other things you'll need to paint the birdhouses and the poles. Yes, paint the poles, too! And don't worry if you make a mess. Just be free and creative. And remember to share your tools with others."

The children painted with dedication for hours, sharing their tools and ideas. Niskala brought them food and juice, and soon she couldn't recognize the children any longer. Their clothes, faces, hair and shoes were covered with paint. She was delighted by their vibrant colors, joy, enthusiasm, and she felt as though she were walking through the world of the childlike soul, nourished by the lightness and innocence of their images. She was so excited to see this side of the human race, the pretty, uplifting, smiling, shining side, unburdened with the human past. Every single creation was unique, peaceful, and without evil, without bad intentions or negative experiences. All this inspired Niskala very much.

When the sun began to set, a colorful flock of birds appeared on the horizon. Brushes and paint buckets froze in little hands, while children followed the descending fleet with open mouths and huge eyes.

"Hey, hey, wake up. Let's finish the birdhouses before they land." Niskala said. "Do you see a hole on the bottom of each birdhouse?" she asked them. "Now, put your birdhouses on the poles that you stuck into the ground, just like this." She showed them and helped the smallest ones who were shorter than the poles. "There you go. You built your birdhouses. Great job!"

Soon, birds landed on each birdhouse, jumping on the roofs, entering through the doors and windows, examining the mirrors and bars inside. The children offered the new visitors food from their palms, and the birds, not afraid, ate from them.

At the end of the day, the children's parents came to take them home. When they saw their children, they were glad Niskala had asked the parents to dress them in old clothes. After everyone was gone, Niskala closed the door on this marvelous day. She climbed up the stairs to her bedroom, took a shower, changed into her nightgown, kissed her sleeping baby, wished the nanny goodnight and went to bed. Like every night, before she closed her eyes, she looked at the small table next to her pillow. There was a bonsai tree underneath a clear dome. On its strong, moss-covered roots was a harmonica—the only thing that remained from Nel. "You will always be alive for me," she said, gently running her palm over the dome. "Good night." She lowered her smiling face to her pillow, remembering a time when they were together, happy, hoping for a better future for everyone.

In the middle of the night, Niskala abruptly opened her eyes and jumped out of the bed. She had had a very strange dream… Looking into the dome with the harmonica, she shook her head as if a silly thought, something impossible had crossed her mind. She returned to bed looking at the harmonica. Then, she got out of the bed, took it and opened it with a screwdriver. Inside was a network of little wooden chambers that looked very much like the corridors and rooms from her dream. She put the harmonica in the light and saw something unreal, unbelievable--a wet trace in one of the chambers. The trace looked just like a tear.

"After so much time? His tear? Still wet?" Immediately, she reassembled the harmonica and put it back next to the tree under the dome. Then she went back to her bed.

"Lacrimal Sea," she whispered, while her hopeful gaze went through the dome into the distance.

She remembered lullabies embroidered with legends. Powerful water, full of mysteries. Each droplet a tear, each grain of sand a crystalized tear, each island a miracle. People came to the shores when they wanted to cry, but couldn't. The sea cried for them, and its waves healed their pain. It could resurrect the dead from the tears they left behind. Those were only legends. But are legends only legends? According to one such story, her tree could preserve things from decaying. And it seemed it really did hold Nel's tear.

"Maybe the Lacrimal Sea exists? But where?" Niskala wondered.

CHAPTER FOUR

REVIVAL AT THE LACRIMAL SEA

Early the next morning, the miller's little daughter opened the door of Niskala's room, slid into her bed, underneath her covers, and then surfaced close to her chin. Holding a feather, she began to tickle her nose. Half-asleep, Niskala was making funny faces that made her burst out laughing. She opened her eyes, of course.

"Niskala, Niskala," she said through her laughter, "wake up, come see."

"I can't," Niskala exclaimed. "Just a little bit longer," she yawned and turned her head to the other side of her pillow.

With a stuffed Koala bear in one hand, the girl managed to pull Niskala out of the bed, and took her to the window.

"Look, Niskala! Look!" In the field, in front of the castle, were myriad birdhouses painted in the most beautiful colors. Birds were flying out of them, like pearls of a necklace connecting to the flock in the sky.

"And where is your birdhouse?" Niskala asked.

"There." She pointed.

"The one with a purple roof?"

"No, the yellow one with an ellipse on the roof."

"Oh, how pretty it is. Imagine when the little birds hatch inside, huh?"

"When is that going to be, Niskala?"

"In the spring, dear. Where is your brother?"

"There he is. With Nafaya." She pointed to a horse in the distance. It seemed as if the two riders had their arms spread and that the birds were landing on them.

"Let's join them. What do you say?" Niskala asked.

"Can we go with them to the mountain? Can we?"

"Of course. It's a gorgeous morning for a long ride." Niskala dressed, went to see Nora, who was asleep in her room, exchanged a few words and smiles with the nanny, and left the castle.

Nearby, the miller and his wife were sitting outside the mill at a small table, drinking their morning coffee, enjoying nature and the sight of the horses and their horsemen. Niskala and the girl in her saddle were riding toward Sunflower Mountain. Right next to them, shoulder-to-shoulder, was Nafaya on his horse, holding the girl's brother in front of him. Judging by his appearance, Nafaya was an old man, but his spirit was unusually lively, and he was always happy like a joyful child. He was bald, with a bit of gray hair on the sides, and he wore John Lennon type glasses that bounced with the movement of the horse. He wore a thin, cream coat and pleated shirt. He supported the arms of the boy who held the reins tightly and seemed to be enjoying the feeling that he was steering the horse alone. They galloped faster and faster through the grass field with yellow flowers, leaving Niskala's castle far behind. On the horizon, they could see a yellow object at the top of the contour of the mountain.

"You have been very reflective the entire morning, dear," Nafaya said to Niskala when they slowed a bit.

"Yes... I had a very strange dream last night. I think it was about Nel. Then I realized that my dream could become reality."

"What do you mean, dear?"

"In my dream, it was night. I saw a rectangular building, and on its façade it read: 'From Niskala with Love.' The building had no roof, just many tiny rooms that I saw from above. It was raining, large drops... they resembled tears. I looked up into the sky and saw a constellation resembling Nel's face. As drops fell into the rooms, I heard notes playing on a harmonica."

"What do you think it means?"

"Remember his harmonica?"

"Yes."

"Well, in the harmonica, in one of the compartments, I found his tear... still wet. Can you believe it?"

"Really?" Nafaya hesitated. "After so many years?"

"I don't know," she shrugged. "It seems it is. Maybe the tree you gave me isn't just a legend after all."

"Wonderful news! What are we waiting for then?" Nafaya took the reins from the boy. "Let's go!" he motioned with his head.

"Where?" Niskala asked.

"To someone who knows where the miracles are, where the Lacrimal Sea is," he said smiling. "Someone who once gave me that same tree as a present."

"Who?"

"You'll see." He responded.

"Nafaya, please tell me. Why are you torturing me? Who is it?" She shook him, making a joke.

"The world became so pretty, my dear, there must be a bit of pain after all," he laughed. "Don't worry. We'll see him on our way to the mountain. I believe he is as old as the world—at least the legend goes something like that. Let's go." Nafaya clicked with his tongue, spurred his horse and gave the reins back to the child. "In the end, everything will be all right. You'll see. All problems are only temporary," he said.

In the distance, the mountain was looming like a giant, and the yellow object was becoming increasingly visible. Close to the top, a huge sunflower was flourishing, sticking its head through the clouds, as though through the windows of a house. They stopped their horses in the valley, and the children stared motionlessly at the petals, as if they could look straight into the sun without having to avert their gazes.

Nafaya pulled out a wooden flute from his bag and played several notes that echoed through the mountain. Suddenly, they heard the humming of the wind, and a reddish, transparent cloak began descending from the top of the mountain, branching into several directions like a gentle spirit spreading its arms towards the visitors. Rustling through the hair of the visitors, the wind appeared to call them to play. It was very gentle, like the finest silk, and the children couldn't stop giggling and scratching their noses and ears. Then, the wind blew so intensely that it lifted the horses from the ground and carried them toward the top of the mountain. The horses turned like a merry-go-round, and the children loved the game and wanted to go faster. As they passed the sunflower, the boy stretched out his arms to touch it, but he was too short.

"Next year," Niskala said, holding him so he would not fall down.

When the mist disappeared, they were on top of the mountain, standing on the edge of a deep crater, holding a group of gray tornadoes. Red Wind approached them, turning as if they were talking about something. At once, the other winds disappeared, and

Red Wind was alone with his guests, turning calmly and patiently in one spot, waiting for the guests to speak to him.

"Good day, Red Wind," Niskala said, bowing her head. The wind was patiently turning. "Nafaya," she said pointing to him, "brought me here to ask you for a favor. I would like so much to revive a friend of mine, but I can't. Can you tell me whether or not the Lacrimal Sea actually exists? I believe it does, and that it can bring him back to life. At least, that is my hope... Wind," she said, taking a few hesitant steps forward, "is there a Lacrimal Sea?"

The wind suddenly disappeared.

"What happened?" Niskala asked Nafaya. He shrugged, equally confused.

"Where did the wind go, Niskala?" The girl asked, while her brother leaned forward and whispered, "Why did the Wind disappear, Niskala?"

As Niskala listened to the children's questions, the Wind returned. It carried something in its whirlpool, some kind of dust. The Wind then became a breeze and gently placed the material on the ground. Niskala dismounted and took some in her hand. It looked like sand.

"Tears?" Many wet, fossilized and crystalized tears glistened on her palm, as she stared at them, utterly surprised.

"It exists?" She lifted her gaze toward the Wind as if waiting for confirmation. The Wind's whirlpool was steadily turning. "It exists!" She exclaimed, looking at the children and Nafaya, who was smiling.

"Thank you, so much, Red Wind. I'm sorry, but I must ask one more favor." The Wind was turning patiently in one spot. "Could you please take me to the Lacrimal Sea, or at least show me the way?" she pleaded. "Please. I hope I can return the favor someday." The Wind moved closer to them, and whirled them into the sky.

Soon they could see Niskala's castle again, and the whirlpool gently landed them right in front of the entrance. The birds left their houses and circled the whirlpool, greeting the Wind with their play. But the Wind did not disappear; it was turning in front of the castle, waiting…

"Niskala," Nafaya put his arm on her shoulder, "I think the Wind wants to take you only. Don't worry about anything; I will take care of Nora and everything else. Just go with the Wind." He hugged her and kissed her on the cheek. She kissed him back.

"Niskala, I don't need the Lacrimal Sea to start my tears. Hurry up now. The Wind is waiting."

Shortly, she came back from her home with a backpack and saddlebags. She patted the children, hugged Nafaya once again, and mounted her horse. They entered the wind's whirlpool that whirled them into the sky.

…

They flew for hours, feeling very secure and comfortable, embraced by the Wind, before it gently placed them on a dried-out riverbed. As it branched into smaller river beds, the Wind guided Niskala through the resulting maze. Eventually, a spectacular image loomed in the distance. Dark clouds filled half of the sky with a gloomy and tense presence. The other half was azure blue, and in the distance a rainbow nestled in the pure, white clouds. The cracked ground below their feet gradually changed to sand, with some shrubs here and there. Niskala stopped her horse and took the sand into her hand. Yes, it was the same sand she had seen back on the mountain; countless shining grains, each of them a miniature tear-shaped crystal and rock. Soon she heard the humming of the waves. Then, from behind a large hill-sized dune, the sea itself emerged. It was immeasurable, stretching to the North, West and East, towards infinity and eternity. To the right, the sea was crystal clear, calm and sparkling. Above, a rainbow bridged the distant islands that merged with the clear sky. To the left, however, the water was rough and wild, whipped with freezing winds and lightning. It seemed a storm would erupt at any second.

Red Wind whirled to the very edge of the shore and moved several inches into the sea. One portion was turning in the rough part of the sea and the other in the part that was calm. The Wind reeled the water up, producing a strange sound, perhaps a language of nature that was completely incomprehensible to Niskala. Then, the whirlpool began to descend, returning the water into the sea. The Wind became a gentle breeze that passed through Niskala and disappeared behind the dunes.

"Thank you so much," she said and steered her horse toward the shore. Images on the calm side called to her and made her want to stay there and rest after her long journey. She cringed and turned away from the gloomy part of the sea and the thundering clouds. The turbulent part of the sea didn't awaken any curiosity in her usually inquisitive mind. Only discomfort.

She pulled back her reins and stopped the horse at the shore of the calm side. The rainbow, the sun that pleasantly warmed her and a soothing breeze were just what she needed. She dismounted and set up her tent on the sand. She took the water container from the saddle-bags, and gave some water to her horse. From the inside pocket of her jacket, she pulled out the harmonica, gently running her thumb over it. She kept doing this for several moments, as if she were touching something deep inside her soul. She stepped forward toward the sea.

"Oh, Lacrimal Sea, between darkness and light, please answer my prayer. Bring Nel back to life from his tear in this harmonica," she pleaded. She waited, feeling her soul fill with hope with every breath as she watched each wave reach the shore.

"Oh, Lacrimal Sea, please answer my prayer and bring Nel back to life. I beg you, sea above all the seas." She bowed down then and kissed the sand. She felt more filled with desire each time she felt how deeply she wanted Nel to return. The Wind continued to blow, the waves hit the shore, but nothing happened.

"Oh sea, above all the seas..." Niskala didn't give up and fell prostrate upon the shore, clutching the harmonica to her heart, waiting and pleading, feeling completely helpless. She felt there was hope for her deepest desire, but she didn't see how she would ever discover the secret key that would let her into the mystery. The sea did not respond. She knew the sea was magical, but maybe her faith was not enough. Was she supposed to do something else too?

As she lay by the sea, a sense of calm came over her. She had offered her true heart's desire to the divine sea, and she believed some help would come to her. And it did after she tried something different, something she hoped would be more appealing to the sea. As she began humming a ballad, the calm water shook with ripples. A fish jumped out, leaving a small wave behind it. A lightning bolt flashed on the other side. Niskala stopped humming, and nature calmed. She began to sing, and another fish jumped, then, a third and a fourth. On the tranquil horizon, the tail of a whale appeared and gently folded itself back into the depth like a fan.

On the rough side, dark nimbus clouds gathered, looking like they would burst at any second. A stream of water shot into the sky, and the whale's tail appeared and vanished once more. A seagull flying toward the rough side transformed into a dark eagle. It shot into a wave and emerged with a spiny fish. A wave pushed the eagle toward the calm side, where it became a seagull once more, dropping the fish into the sea. The fish was no longer covered in its spiky armor but rather shone with intense colors, its sleek body glistening in the sun.

Mesmerized, Niskala stopped her melody, and the gull disappeared. Sitting in the sand, holding the harmonica in her lap, she began to sing more while observing the serene horizon. It would be wonderful, she thought, if everything went smoothly. She envisioned her love standing in front of her in the sand, preparing a wooden boat, with oars and room for only the two of them. Overwhelmed with joy, she saw them sailing along the pleasant side of the sea. But the roar of thunder shook her, and she began to wonder what would really happen next. What if the rough side were to awaken even more?

Suddenly, a horseman appeared on the horizon, galloping through the water towards Niskala. The horse's hooves were hitting the surface of the water with intense power, as if it were solid ground. Wearing silver armor but no helmet, the horseman was rapidly approaching. His long blond hair and the horse's white mane were swept back by the air. The sound of the armor was loud, louder than the noise of the waves from the other side. He rode straight toward Niskala. A few steps away from her, the horse reared on the surface of the sea, not out of anger or fear, but in greeting.

Niskala stood up and stepped into the water. Now, she could make out his strong facial features. His eyes were not yet clearly visible, but she felt his gaze, a source of unrelenting trust. He did not look aside or speak. He only nodded slightly, as if to greet Niskala.

"Who are you?" she asked.

He didn't say anything, just raised his arm, and a hawk materialized on it. The bird flew to Niskala, took the harmonica from her hand, and landed on the arm of his lord. The horseman pulled the reins, turned his horse, and galloped into the distance. As the horseman merged with the horizon, a gray-blue wave began to roll toward the shore. Closer to the shore, the wave became smaller. It was carrying something. A new wave emerged and took over the cargo. When this wave became powerless, it surrendered its cargo to the next one. It was something pale. Carried from wave to wave, a lifeless, naked body was turning. The next wave briefly uncovered its face: it was Nel! A few more waves, and he was lying in the sand on the shore of fossilized tears.

Niskala got a blanket from her bag, quickly approached the body and turned it. It was him! Nel! Her Nel! Why were his eyes closed? Was he asleep? Was he alive? She was looking for even the tiniest sign of life. Seconds ticked like hours. She searched for his pulse and felt the faint heartbeat. Was she imagining it? Then, she saw the movement of his chest—he was breathing! An indescribable joy and relief overwhelmed her. Niskala smiled. He was alive! Alive! She threw herself on his body, hugging and kissing him on the face, hair and shoulders. Tears of joy and relief poured down her face, and she leaned her ear against his heart, listening to the comforting sound of his awakening.

"Oh, sea above all seas, thank you so much for granting my wish. I am eternally thankful," Niskala said bowing her head.

She watched Nel, quietly and with infinite tenderness, as he slept. She gently ran her hand through his hair tangled with algae. Through transparent grains on his eyelashes, Nel saw something sublime, as if he were observing a scene in paradise through a stained-glass window. Those dear fingers, the nail polish, glass beads and a silver starfish on her anklet... But was this real? He was so confused... his last memories were about a wish he had... to touch his harmonica, a present from Niskala... in the world ruled by a regime that he despised and attempted to run away from... his escape wasn't successful... he was lying on something hard and cold... with his arms tied to it... tears rolled down his cheek... the harmonica slid from his shirt pocket towards his face... the harmonica touched his face and dropped to the floor... and that's where the memories abruptly stopped.

But this... what was this now? Something like a fairy-tale... Was he dead? Was he alive? He tried to move his arm to reach for the foot he remembered so well, with that starfish anklet … but he didn't have enough strength for it. With nostalgia, he now remembered everything about Niskala... Still in disbelief, he somehow managed to lift his head slightly. Niskala spread her arms open. "I am here, my love," she said smiling, reaching for her dearest Nel. "We are together again."

A flood of sunlight shone from her straight into his face, and his head fell into the sand again. "I missed you… the Sun of my life," he thought. She leaned towards him and kissed his hair, imagining his hand touching her face, like before. But he had already fallen asleep…

CHAPTER FIVE

BEAUTY OF EMBODIED TRUTH

Several years later.

Where a sunflower field changed into a field of red poppies, Niskala and Nel stopped their horses. In the saddle, Nel held five-year-old Nora while Io, Niskala's son, was riding in her saddle. He was eight. They were attracted to a large group of people who were sitting in the field, motionlessly listening to a young woman around twenty years of age. In a white robe, she stood in front of the crowd, telling them a story. The listeners were mesmerized. They closed their eyes as they listened and wide smiles appeared on their relaxed faces, like they were in some type of a trance. Nobody even noticed Niskala, since if they had, they would've run towards her to touch and hug her. No one would want to miss an opportunity to come closer to her—this wise, warm, approachable leader, with amazing accomplishments, she was admired by all. They loved Nel too, but for them, he was more of a ray of light, while she was the Sun.

Niskala, Nel, and the children approached the group from behind, quietly, trying not to disturb the apparent harmony of something very significant, an event resembling a spiritual gathering between a teacher and her followers. The young woman noticed them, smiled warmly in their direction, but only for a moment. She returned her gaze once again to her audience, so as not to disturb the continuity of a positive mood that everyone seemed to share. She wanted to give as much as possible of herself to her audience. To everyone present, it was clear that she had the skill of transporting people into a world of stories and legends. She was telling them what happened after the Lacrimal Sea resurrected Nel.

"...and then Nel asked Niskala," the woman said. "These wings that your friend Icarus created are truly marvelous. But, what's their use? I mean, I don't see any application other than a means of transportation. For me, however, wings have always had a symbolic function." Nel raised his hand, depicting a flight toward heaven. "They represent freedom, breaking shackles, moving away from values that are obsolete, expanding one's consciousness, experiencing new horizons... improving oneself... progress of the human race... connecting with the universe... reaching a higher spiritual plane of existence... becoming enlightened... moving away from materialism... At least that's how it is in my art," Nel said.

The woman stopped for a moment, glancing over the transfixed faces in the audience, noticing all that positive energy coming from them, stimulating her to continue:

"I know. For me, too," Niskala agreed. "I don't even want everyone to have wings right now. Just you, Icarus, and the children."

"Just us?" Asked Nel.

"I'd like it so much if the two of you would teach them to fly. But not just to move their wings mechanically. Anyone could do that without a teacher. I'd like for them to learn what the sky is and how wide it is. To sense what clouds are, to breathe them in, fill their lungs with them, to be friends with them. To come closer to the stars. To look at the earth from another perspective. Besides, I'd like them to never forget that earth is their home, and that the sky is just their temporary sanctuary. That would be the best birthday present for me." She sighed, placing her head on his shoulder.

"Wonderful!" he said, running his fingers through her hair. "You and your sweet dreams. You have no idea how much I love to be a part of them. Do you really think I can teach children how to fly? I've never done something like that."

"Oh, I'm certain you can do it. You are an artist. You fly to heaven every day, to that world of inspiration and creativity. In that intoxicating world you are not limited by anything, yet you always manage to return to earth, to its ordinary reality of constraints and responsibilities, adjusting to it so well. I'm sure you can also teach children how to do the same," the storyteller said, happy that her audience was clearly mesmerized by her tale.

With a large smile, Niskala and Nel remembered those moments when, acknowledging Niskala's wish, Nel taught children to fly. The oral tradition, the stories about their lives and their adventures existed; however, nobody could recount those events in such an extremely vivid, vibrant way until this woman told her story. Everyone, including Nel and Niskala, was completely intoxicated with her story-telling which transported them from an everyday reality into the world of their past, as if the past were happening here and now, so clearly and accurately.

It was obvious that the story-teller had an immense gift, a rare and special one. The movements of her body—posture, facial grimacing, enthusiasm, word emphases, dramatic pauses, hand gestures, the pleasantness of her voice and the proper pace of speech—all that was mixed into a perfect flow of effortless creativity and communication. With amazement, Nel attentively followed the woman's every word. Niskala observed him with enjoyment, understanding his nostalgia for the period of his life where adventures had been abundant. Although parts of those adventures were not at all wonderful, sometimes they were dangerous and bitter and painful, but what he valued the most was the discovery of solutions to puzzles and mysteries. These discoveries were priceless. And he missed them, a lot. Niskala was deeply touched that someone showed up who could so remarkably convey the truth, without subjective interpretation and additions of story elements that never happened. In Niskala's eyes, the woman was the embodiment of truth.

Niskala glanced over hundreds of smiles, relaxed bodies and dreamy eyes filled with joy and serenity. She was moved by how mesmerized people were, as if the storyteller entranced them with some good magic. And then she began to sing a song about the sky, an ode to it. Her angelic voice spread like a wave through the field, making the red flowers vibrate and move. Everyone felt her voice deep inside, touching their souls, gently connecting them with everything there was—other people, insects, birds, flowers, clouds, the Sun. Everything became one: Perfect harmony. Niskala could only utter: "Ah," while Nel struggled not to cry, moved by something so beautiful and transcendent, so unique and divine-like. Io and Nora, as if drawn by gravity, cut their way through the crowd and sat in the first row, wanting to be as close as possible to the storyteller.

"What an angel." Nel said to Niskala.

"Yes. With her, a great day became even better. What do you think about inviting her to Heliopolis? I think she would make it even greater and more powerful with her presence. Don't you think?"

"Absolutely!" Nel exclaimed. "She would connect with people so well in its parks."

"Great idea. So be it then," Niskala responded with a smile.

The gathering was coming to a close, and the woman said to her audience: "Light emanates from us, by the way of our virtues..."

She paused and looked at the people, who nodded. "We all know that those are Niskala's words, and it is never enough to hear her wisdom, but for today, these were her last words and mine. If you like, you can come back here tomorrow at the same time, and I will tell you how Icarus and Nel taught children to fly, and what they discovered in the sky. I wish you a wonderful day, and I can't wait to see you tomorrow," she said with a big smile on her face, waving to the crowd.

As she spoke her parting words, everyone rushed to her, to touch and greet her, impatiently waiting for another great day with her. She firmly hugged every single person, with a big smile on her face, and everyone could feel her field of immense warmth and authenticity. Then, a surprise... People noticed Niskala, who was about to approach the woman. Everyone was elated. What an incredible day! First, the amazing storyteller, then Niskala. They didn't know whom to greet first.

Niskala wanted to greet the woman, but since she felt that people needed her, she postponed her wish for later. Those who were hugged by the storyteller, made a few steps to Niskala to be hugged by her too—a very special sight indeed: Two extraordinary women standing next to each other, attracting people who needed them both. There was something very similar about their energy, about how these women smiled and moved, how people loved them, and standing next to one another, greeting people, it was like there was a mirror between them, where one woman's charisma was a reflection of the other's. To Nel it was as clear as day that Niskala and the storyteller were similar, that there was an invisible bridge between them, that they would soon become friends, likely the best of friends, perhaps even soulmates, and he couldn't wait to see how this connection was going to develop.

When people left, Niskala approached the woman, hugged her and said, "It was incredible what you did today. You are born to gather people and fill them with happiness. I have never seen anything like this."

"That was amazing," Nel added. "I'm speechless."

"Thank you. Thank you so much," she said. "What an honor that you are here. Thank you Niskala, Nel, Nora, and Io for being a part of today." She patted the children.

"What is your name?" asked Niskala.

"Adiana," the woman replied.

"Mom..." Nora was pulling Niskala's arm. "Can Adiana come to our home? We can't wait to show her our rooms. Please, mommy?"

"Of course," Niskala said. "Whenever she wants. And one more thing, Adiana... would you like to come to Heliopolis, to do what you did here today? Whenever you want. You can do it every day if you like."

"Absolutely! I would love that!" said Adiana without hesitation. "Thank you, Niskala; this is the best day of my life yet." She hugged Niskala very firmly.

"You're welcome. Heliopolis will be enriched with your presence," Niskala said.

"I have visited it so many times, admiring everything about it. I never thought about being invited to contribute to its glory. And by the great Niskala herself. What an honor," Adiana said.

"The honor is mine. So, when shall we expect you there?" Niskala asked.

"The day after tomorrow. I can't go tomorrow since I promised the people that I would tell them another story here. But, the day after tomorrow, I'll come to Heliopolis." Io and Nora were jumping with joy.

"Wonderful! We can't wait to see you again," Niskala exclaimed. "What a beautiful way to end the day. Come here all of you!" Niskala spread her arms and hugged them all at once including Adiana. In that gesture, Adiana felt that she was welcomed into Niskala's family, and she was so happy that she was becoming a part of it.

...

The next day, in the field of red poppies, the number of people doubled. They could not wait to hear Adiana—the amazing storyteller. When she showed up, a standing ovation followed for several minutes. She stood there in front of them, smiling and eventually gestured, inviting them to sit down. Then she told them this story:

"On the top of Sunflower Mountain, covered with long stalks of wheat, stood Icarus. In his arms he held a little girl with big brown eyes. Her chin was on the shoulder of his dark blue cashmere coat, her eyes following the orange ball in the sky. Nearby, was a lighthouse, and over the edge of the mountain, far below the gigantic sunflower, a spacious lake. As the wind passed, Icarus's collar suddenly rose, attaching to his neck, and the girl's hair trembled. A redheaded boy was standing next to them on a rock, moving his eyeglasses up and down, trying to get Icarus's attention. Icarus sat on the rock, placed the girl next to him, and put the boy on his lap, hugging them both, staring into the sky.

"The rest of the children giggled as they tried to lift Nel from the ground, where he lay with his arms behind his head. He pretended to be asleep. They put wheat in his hair, making it appear like the sun they were watching. When the wheat tickled his nose, his lip twitched into a half-smile, which he quickly hid. Icarus touched a sphere on the front of his jacket; it recognized his finger print, and a pair of wings unfolded on his back from a disc.

"Look, look, Icarus is flying! Icarus is flying!" The children were jumping up to touch his feet. He flew over the nearby steps and entered the lighthouse. Suddenly, they could hear humming, and a powerful light beam shot straight into heaven.

"When are we going to fly? We want to fly, too. Now! Now!"

"Just a few more minutes," Icarus said.

"Let's get you ready!" Nel said to the children touching spheres on their jackets, activating their wings. Icarus pulled a wool cap with a chip over each child's head. The chip could detect one's intention to fly, transmitting that signal to the wing's mechanism. He and Nell put gloves on the children's hands and sunblock on their faces. They arranged the children into two groups. One led by Icarus, the other by Nel.

"Now, take my right hand," Icarus said to one of the children, "and give your other hand to the next child. Just like that. The rest of you do the same. Good job! And you, you can take my left hand and give your empty hand to him. There you go. The rest of you do the same." Icarus was arranging the children into two lines that intersected at the top where he was. Nel did the same with his group of children.

"When we are in the sky, in case you drop someone's hand, don't worry. Just think about coming back to us or say it, and your wings will obey. Even if you don't issue any command, they are programmed to take you to Nel or myself. We'll be right next to you."

"Kids, have a look at the lighthouse," Nel explained. "Whenever we tell you so, you need to look into its beam and follow it with your gaze to the lighthouse. Why is this important? Anyone?"

"To know where the earth is," one of the girls answered.

"Exactly," Nel responded. "If we don't know where the earth is, we'll get lost in the sky. The sky is gorgeous, but dangerous if we aren't careful. Like too much ice cream in a single day! Now, do you understand all this?" Nel asked.

"Yes, we do," the children sang in unison.

"Excellent, then. Without further ado, let's fly!" Icarus said, and they rose above the ground holding their hands, and the children followed after him.

"Hurray! Hurray! We're flying! This is terrific!" The children were excited. Only the last child in each line had one empty hand, waving to the earth and to the birds they were meeting as they flew up.

In the sky, on their left, within a cloud, a myriad of droplets were approaching, bouncing against each other without any apparent order, creating scattered, abstract foggy shapes. But, the orange light that had just emerged from behind a cloud illuminated that beautiful chaos, and the children discovered in it a new, orderly world. The rays of light revealed miniature symmetrical units, tiny squares, circles and triangles, belonging to the bigger ones. It was obvious that a hidden connection and structure had always existed among these seemingly disconnected and disorganized parts. It only took light and a different perspective to see the yet unseen.

They looked below, towards the earth, into the numerous, tiny lights, appearing and disappearing, coming from streets, homes, stores and vehicles. But the children did not see only that; in all those sparks that were vanishing and returning, they saw something more--a story about magic that happens when the pieces of a whole belong and work together to make the entire scene extraordinarily beautiful, breathtaking. In all that light they experienced the magic of unity and togetherness of themselves, Nel and Icarus, of Niskala and all the people.

Looking below his feet, through the mists of the dissipating clouds, Nel saw the vast mass of unified land and water—the surface of the earth. Why would someone invent borders, he wondered, ruining the pristine beauty and the mesmerizing oneness of nature? Why impose some imaginary, unnecessary lines of division? It was very easy to see, from that perspective and altitude, that earth was meant to be shared; it was a sacred medium meant to bridge gaps and connect, not something that should be broken into pieces, into territories proclaimed to be someone's possessions, bordering on what belongs to others. Here in the sky, that idea stared him in the face--that borders and divisions should have never existed, that countries should be unified instead, that people should live in harmony, celebrating their differences, not allowing these qualities to divide them. Yet, he recalled history, people opposing that sublime oneness of nature, bringing disharmony and ruin to it, and to each other. They imposed their own vision of how things should be, how all of nature should appear, how all things could and should be conquered, constrained, modified, enslaved and exploited.

The sky landscape was just right, so reflections continued pouring out of Nel… Niskala turned all that was wrong around, correcting it—her borderless world was a reflection of the sanctity of connectedness. Various traditions and cultures, the richness of their diversity--they were protected in her world without borders, respected, nurtured and glorified. And in that unifying plane of existence, each individual was its valuable citizen, embraced by it and embracing it. It should have been like that from the dawn of civilization, but what was missing, Nel realized, were leaders with the ability to lift off the ground and soar to the sky. Flying through heaven would have helped them attain a different perspective, one which gives birth to a vision that unifies people and pulls the best out of them. The skill of flying, unfortunately, was unknown to them, and learning to fly was something they believed only birds were supposed to do. Hence, Nel realized their "creativity" was lacking uniqueness, novelty and usefulness for humankind. And once these essential ingredients are missing, how can true creativity even arise? Niskala, however, knew how to fly. She was an expert at it. In landing too. He smiled. Thinking about her always made him do so.

In the distance, stretching across the entire horizon was a wall of granite-colored clouds. As they approached one of the clouds, its empty space grew larger, as if a heavy gate opened.

"Let's go! Let's go through it!" The children were excited.

The oval window in the "granite wall" was slowly closing, yet it was still wide enough to let them through. As Nel was flying through the cloud, the transition from gray to several darker shades of gray dazzled him with the resemblance to a layered monolith. As he touched the dark mass, he felt its coldness, distance, and age. It felt hard as stone, like the wall of a temple full of mysteries. He glanced at the children, concerned that they could injure themselves against the stone. Then, seeing the cobweb-like texture disappearing on his palm, he remembered that it was just a cloud. He understood. The monolith was just a powerful illusion created by his altered consciousness, induced by this intoxicating flight.

On the other side of the "tunnel," above the orange horizon, Nel saw Icarus hovering in one spot, his back straight as an arrow, completely mute, his head raised even higher. Still holding the hands of the children, he bent his arms slightly at the elbow as if he were praying. His wings were calmly beating in the rhythm of a meditation.

"What's going on in the seventh heaven?" Nel asked in a loud voice to attract attention. He was afraid that Icarus had forgotten that children couldn't control their imaginations that well.

"Here we are!" He spoke loudly again. Everyone from Icarus's group finally turned toward him and his children, calling them to join.

"Children, look at the beam from the lighthouse. It's over there." Icarus pointed with his head. "Follow it with your gaze to find the lighthouse. Earth is our home," Icarus said. "It's our destination. We'll only be traveling through the sky sometimes, to relax and get inspired."

"Like when we go to our summer houses?" A child remarked.

"Exactly. Only sometimes," Icarus said. "The sky will help us live on our beautiful earth, to get ideas of how to improve our life down there. We won't leave our home and move to the sky, though. We can get lost in this limitless vastness. Some day, I'll tell you the story of how I got lost in the sky when I was a young, foolish boy." The children giggled at "foolish."

"Look! Look!" the children were saying. At such height, down below, through the drifting clouds, they saw no more roads, streets, bridges, or houses, only motionless lines scattered all over the dark plate. The surface of the earth looked insignificant, dull, and barren. And then, in a split second, when the sunlight shone upon the earth, all that changed--all those lines, sleepy and unimportant, began to look like golden stalks of wheat, waving in the wind, touching each other silently and gently. The shadowy, abandoned plate became a fertile, golden field.

Icarus and the children silently observed the miraculous transformation. However, Nel couldn't understand what they saw down there. What was so interesting in lifeless lines and dots on the dark plate that suddenly illuminated? He confusedly glanced at Icarus, who was explaining something to the children.

"Now, dear flyers, look up into the sky and see what's going on up there." Everyone looked up.

"Unforgettable, isn't it?" Icarus said, raising his sunglasses. Nel could easily see the huge yellow sphere, levitating on the horizon to their left, and he admired it, but higher in the sky he couldn't see anything other than the elongated yellow clouds and the blue sky. Actually, it seemed a bit funny to him that Icarus was elated by things like that. Nature was gorgeous, okay, but not so spectacular as to throw someone into the trance that everyone around him was in. It must be that none of them really knew the nature of ultimate artistic heights, he mused.

For Icarus and the children, however, elongated yellow clouds looked like intensifying flames touching the azure ocean. Long streaks of fire were burning through the water. Perfect peace, without sizzling or the slightest indication of conflict. Fire and water together, in an inspiring connection, like best friends, or lovers romantically embraced. Nel saw children's faces covered with unexplainable calm, amazement, and joy. He saw that Icarus and the children experienced this flight on a much deeper level than he could. For the rest of them, heaven and its elements became an entrance into another dimension, yet, in Nel's eyes, all that unfolded in the sky was a beautiful matter, lifeless and ordinary. But why couldn't he also become a part of this deeper, more complete experience, he wondered. Shouldn't he too be granted a passage into that hidden world? Wasn't he entitled to it, didn't he deserve it, as a brilliant artist who inspired millions? What happened to him? He couldn't understand.

Everyone looked to Icarus and enjoyed his explanations. Everyone else seemed to belong to the same world of imagination and connectedness with one another. Nel looked into tiny hands that he held in his, yet he felt disconnected from them, alone. He was terrified.

"What is going on?" he muttered, feeling expelled from heaven, without knowing the reason. His soul felt so distant now, severed from him and taken away.

For the entire, long week, he felt the same—unrecognizable to himself, alienated from his identity, lost. If only he shared how he felt with Niskala, perhaps she would have helped him somehow. Something was deeply troubling him, she felt, but he did not let her in, dismissing his feeling as temporary weakness, denying its weight and impact. But the feeling rapidly worsened, exacerbated, and overwhelmed him completely.

...

Late one evening, piercing the silence with the clapping of his wings, he returned alone back to Sunflower Mountain. His mission: unknown. Perhaps to tear it down with his meaninglessness. Oh, there was enough pain, helplessness, and anger for that. His eyes were without any spark of life, the sky moonless, starless... Lonely lighthouse, in the distance, enveloped with darkness... The bridges towards salvation painted black... just as if they never existed. Inside him there was a labyrinth without a thread to follow. All around, only darkness.

His soul was stolen... as if he was being punished... But for what? Transgressions? What were they? Was he an innocent victim, perhaps? He was entrapped by an evil spell... a spell that devoured all that was original and useful in him. Where was the evil coming from, when there wasn't any on Earth any longer? From his own depth? No... This evil wasn't his... He knew himself all too well... his soul wasn't there any longer. The evil had been done to him. Someone or something was against him. But not of this world, definitely not... this world was good, Niskala's world. What then? His thoughts ended at the beginning of his wheel of thinking.

The contours of his fragile shadow that hovered and trembled above the gigantic sunflower were misleading. He was far away from being gentle and quiet like a hummingbird. His entire body was shaking, gazing with sorrow through the flower... he couldn't understand it. In the past he would have been able to, but not any longer. Now, the flower was just a flower... something alive, something pretty... and transient. Yet, the gentle being of the sunflower was looking at him with its enameled glitter, moving its petals as if it were calling him to come closer... to listen... it was whispering to him in the quiet tongue of the breeze... telling him what to do... how to regain his soul... but, he couldn't hear the words, just some humming and the noise of petals moving in the wind. In the past, he would have been able to understand that hidden language of nature, but not anymore.

As he landed on the mountain, his wings calmed and retracted. He was left without his home and hut, without his expression. Only through creativity could he exist--through his prints, sculptures, and poetry. If only he could create again. But nothing could inspire him. Why? Oh, why when the conditions were just right for a life fulfilled with yet unseen creations? Why? There was so much of all that joyful gentleness, understanding, positivity, and the events that had surrounded him since he was resurrected from his tear. So much love and optimism all around. The spirit of humanism had finally enveloped Earth. Yet, for him, that new renaissance became his downfall. He looked at himself with scorn, disgusted by what he had become.

The erosion took everything away... it even tore Niskala from his heart. He did not love her anymore. Some mysterious catastrophe stole everything sublime from him, leaving behind only questions without answers, questions, heavy like mountains collapsing over him and entrapping him, tying him to the ground. How was he happy in the past that was full of wars and hatred, yet here he was sinking through sorrow in this enlightened future that he and Niskala had envisioned?

"Will I ever reclaim my soul? Will I ever be able to fly again?" He nostalgically remembered his encounter with the wings when Niskala showed them to him for the first time. That was Icarus's prototype, the one Nel further improved with his artistic design. He recalled numerous sleepless nights that he spent making them their gorgeous, perfect shape, painted just right, with images telling amazing stories. He remembered when he finished them, how everyone was awe-struck, including Icarus and Niskala. He recalled Icarus' words that all three of them gave life to wings—Niskala with her support, Icarus contributed scientifically and Nel with his art.

"My creator... The Lacrimal Sea...," he muttered looking into the distance. "It must know what happened to my soul," he said, as if a sudden light shone through the darkness of his world. He pressed the sphere on his jacket, his wings unfolded.

"Towards the Lacrimal Sea," he commanded, and the wings took him high into the sky.

Adiana's audience was ready for more, but that's where Adiana decided to stop, and said:

"If you'd like to hear what happened to Nel next, I'll continue the story next Monday in Heliopolis. So join me there! Until then I wish you a great time."

"We love you. We love you," people were shouting, approaching her to say goodbye.

CHAPTER SIX

HELIOPOLIS

Shaped like a dome, composed of a myriad of white spheres and mirror-coated windows, with a diameter of 500 meters and the surface of around 30 soccer fields, Heliopolis was a graceful colossus of modern architecture. However, its most significant feature was how it affected people. It could change them, improve them. Spending time in Heliopolis, a person would become younger, healthier, gain a better span of attention and focus. One would be able to better analyze and solve problems and make better decisions in life. Further, a person would become more creative and ethical. Heliopolis could make people wiser.

Change in social behavior would be apparent as well in Heliopolis—people would cooperate more with others, show more respect and less prejudice than before. Also, people would be able to better notice someone's suffering, and they would more often offer help. But that wasn't all that happened in Heliopolis; in addition to developing love towards others, people learned to love themselves. People were better able to express and understand their emotions, to control them; at the same time, they were able to reduce, or even eliminate, the negative feelings. People would be able to identify emotions in others with more accuracy, and, as a result, better understand their causes. Heliopolis also nurtured spirituality, developing tolerance of various religions in its visitors. To people who would step into this city for the first time, it would soon become apparent how Heliopolis was accomplishing such change. In it, there was an abundance of music and light, parks with lush vegetation, sport courts, children's playgrounds, pools and jacuzzis. All of these amenities influenced individuals to feel better, to relax and to stimulate their senses with pleasing sounds, intoxicating scents, caressing touches of warm water and massage therapists, mesmerizing light-effects and breathtaking architectural sights. But, that was only the beginning—only the first stage of the city's influence. At another level, people were able to experience Heliopolis's pyramids and domes.

In the pyramids, teachers shared their knowledge about how to be a good parent. Teachers also instructed visitors on proper diet and healthy food preparation, how to recognize others' distress and offer help, how to use mental exercises for improving one's mood, how to meditate, how to love oneself without being conceited and self-absorbed, how to establish a fulfilling romantic relationship based on similarities between the partners, and how to reach for the forgotten inner child who brings innocence, curiosity, inspiration, creativity, playfulness, and mindfulness without worry. Some pyramids were dedicated to massage, bringing relaxation to people's bodies and minds.

In domes, people could develop a deeper appreciation of art, sculpture, live music, and dance. Also, they could engage in physical exercise and experience comical performances, stimulating them to smile and laugh. In addition, domes nurtured religious tolerance as well as appreciation of customs, values, and geographical locations of various cultures in the world. As Niskala would put it, Heliopolis was a temple that nourished the light of our virtues. This city was an epicenter of positive energy, which applied the scientific research that positive thoughts and feelings have like effects on all aspects of one's life.

Of all Niskala's contributions to the progress of humanity, it can be said that building Heliopolis was one of the most important ones. However, she did not treat her deeds as final. No, she would try to improve everything she created; she always saw room for it. Thus, she thought that Adiana's engagement in Heliopolis would further enhance its influence on people. And that's exactly what happened. Instantaneously, Adiana became a main attraction. In whichever park she showed up, delivering her exceptional stories, that location became the most visited that day. In whichever Heliopolis she would appear--since there were many Heliopolises throughout the world-- that particular Heliopolis would become the most visited on the planet.

It is difficult to say what it was about Adiana that made her so charismatic and magnetizing for people. Was it her physical appearance, resembling an angel? Or, was it her singing voice that made such a deep impression on people's souls, without ever leaving them? With her speech and body language, she could portray anything—rain, mist, a willow, a butterfly, a bear, metamorphosis... with that skill, she could easily teleport people to the heart of the story she was telling. Her eyes were overflowing with hope, spontaneity, innovation, determination, courage, affection, and intelligence, and it was obvious that she was a happy person. Probably the most attractive part of her was a desire to transfer her positive energy onto everyone in her audience. And she was so successful in that.

Those who came to Heliopolis to hear her, left feeling transformed—she was a life-changing experience. Adiana was a Heliopolis within the Heliopolis—exactly what Niskala aimed to accomplish with it. She wanted everyone to become an embodiment of this amazing city. Many did attain that goal, but it would not be an exaggeration to say that Adiana went "a mile" further than everyone else. The beauty of her virtues and skills was on a completely different level, a much higher one.

There was nothing that Niskala could pass onto Adiana from a treasury of her wisdom, to make Adiana become even wiser. In Niskala's eyes, she was already a precious gem, unable to be polished any further. Niskala was impressed that Adiana was so young, barely twenty, yet she had the wisdom of someone who was a thousand years old. If, for some reason, the time came for Niskala to withdraw from the role of leader, she would, undoubtedly, recommend Adiana as her successor. Everyone knew that.

At the point where two parks would have touched, there was a wide wall separating them. Using the stairs, Adiana quickly reached the top of the wall, to see everybody from both parks. Metal spheres flew towards her; they were cameras, displaying her image on the levitating video beams so that everyone in Heliopolis could see her.

"Dear people," Adiana said, "so far you and I have been sharing wonderful moments in the field of red poppy flowers. Today, however, we meet here. This location, Heliopolis, is one of the most important architectural creations ever made. We see it as a sacred site. It has deeply touched the hearts and minds of all of us. It has changed our lives and improved us. But, not so many people know the story about how Niskala came up with the idea to erect the wonder where we stand today. Let me tell you that story." And so, she began:

"In our recent history, there was a time, when nightmares plagued humanity. Everything collapsed since people were extremely tired, due to lack of sleep. It was crucial to block genes causing nightmares, but no one knew how to do that. Niskala didn't know either, until she walked on a road to inspiration...

Beneath her feet were tiny pebbles on a road that went around a small, inhabited island. She saw a boy and a girl, sitting in the middle of the road, playing with transparent figurines, shaped like pyramids and domes. With a branch, pressing in the pebbles, they drew a circle, and in it, placed the figurines in an upright position. The girl ran to a nearby bush, took a few branches of lavender and rosemary and inserted them, here and there, among the circle's pebbles.

"These will be our trees." She said. The boy liked the idea and picked more branches, placing them with the rest. They noticed Niskala approaching, left everything, and ran towards her.

"Come, Niskala, play with us. Let's play."

"What game are you playing?" She asked, hugging them.

"We are building a very special place," the boy said.

"Really? What makes it so special?" Niskala asked.

"Its magic can repair broken dolls," the girl said, pointing to her broken dolls scattered around.

"And broken marbles," the boy added, pulling out of his pocket a few chipped ones.

"Very special place, indeed," Niskala responded.

She sat next to the children, helping them fix several trees in the circle that fell. Then, more children arrived, and, since everyone wanted to sit next to her, she promised she would stand up every few minutes and sit next to each child. They liked that idea very much.

"Can you let me borrow your Sun?" A boy asked Niskala, pointing to the Sun pendant on her necklace. "But only the Sun, not those other things."

"Of course." She took the Sun pendant off, gave it to him, and he placed it into the middle of the circle.

More children arrived from their homes on the hill and joined them at play.

"Would you like some?" A boy asked. "These snacks are very healthy, my mom says." Healthy food or not, all children came to him. He handed one to Niskala who tasted it.

"Delicious! This is really something, you know? I already feel much healthier. I'll have to ask your mom for the recipe," Niskala said, making him feel very good and proud.

A girl ran to the sea, and scooped some water with her doll's cups and plates. "These will be jacuzzis and swimming pools. To rest in them after school and homework." She handed one by one to Niskala who placed them into the circle.

"Can you put these in too? Under domes and pyramids." A boy handed a few marbles to Niskala, and she placed them where he said.

Hours passed in their play, and it was amazing to see how easily children accepted adult Niskala as one of them. Sitting with them there, participating, she did not stand out in any way; it was as if she became a child too. A little boy lost something that he wanted to contribute to their circle, so he started crying. Niskala put him on her lap and wiped his tears, giving him her bracelets. That quickly cheered him up, especially when he placed them into the circle with the rest of the items that were enticing him. Other children placed flowers into them. "These will be our parks," a girl said.

Niskala gave them her ring and earrings with tiny mirrors reflecting light. They loved the game of reflecting light on each other and Niskala; then, they patiently positioned the earrings into the circle, illuminating the precious objects in there.

Suddenly, Niskala's face changed. She became distant and very focused on what she was building with the children, to the extent that only that creation seemed to exist for her. Everything else vanished from her mind: the island, the children, the sounds they were making, the crickets, the smells, the pine trees, everything. All, but the circle and the things in it. She saw something in what they were creating, something so important... In those seconds of inspiration, she saw a solution that may save humankind. Her absence lasted briefly, merely a few seconds, but when she returned from that realization, a large smile graced her face.

She closed her eyes, inhaled deeply, and exhaled. Her body and face became calm, as if a huge burden fell off her shoulders. She gently stood up and for a few moments looked into the distance... into the horizon above the sea, the sky, and back again to the island and children. Standing above them, she touched the closest child on his head and extended her palm, calling him with her nod to take it. She patted a girl and extended her palm too. Holding Niskala's hands, they silently stood up and followed her, while she smilingly looked at the rest of them, calling them all with the movement of her head. All of the children began standing up, one by one, and soon the entire group of them walked joyfully behind Niskala, following her. Other children began coming out of their houses, joining this procession. The group was becoming larger and larger as more children joined.

Parents were on the windows and porches, pronouncing Niskala's name with smiles and admiration. Yet, they did not join the procession... They felt that the gathering was not about them, at least not for now. In that gathering of children and Niskala, they felt a powerful flow of youthfulness, understanding, togetherness, and love—

something that was perfect on its own, self-sustained, and should not be altered or disturbed in any way. Niskala stopped walking and the children did the same. She wiped her tears of happiness, relief, and gratitude. With a big smile, she turned towards the children and said:

"Thank you dear children! You helped me tremendously today. You helped all of us, actually. If only I could hug you all at once." She then turned towards parents, "And thank *you* for all of these wonderful children." Then she spoke to the children again: "You are the *key* to our great success today. You gave me an idea of immeasurable importance. In our play, I found inspiration."

Then she spoke to the parents: "Come, walk with us. Let's celebrate! This is the day when Heliopolis begins to rise. A place where nightmares will stop. For all of us!" Children sang and danced around with Niskala, hugging and kissing her. Parents flocked to the gathering, merging with children and Niskala, who led that fairly large group several times around the island.

This is the day when Heliopolis begins to rise..." Those words echoed in everyone. Nobody, except Niskala, knew at that point what exactly she meant by it. The only thing everyone was certain about, however, was that it would be something able to heal them with its light.

With those words Adiana finished the story. A musician, carrying a guitar, had just exited a dome, curious to hear the storyteller that everyone was talking about lately. Adiana made a hand-gesture calling him... She whispered something in his ear with a big smile on her face... He laughed and nodded, lending her his guitar. That was exactly what made her so special—her creativity was spontaneous, unpredictable. Although the twists and turns of her storytelling, and the means that she used to deliver them, were impossible to predict, everyone could rest assured that the story endings would be joyful, with a mood-lifting message for all. Sometimes, she would use a hat or a belt or something else belonging to a person from her audience; sometimes, she would ask a listener, or more of them, to join her, but this time, that guitar caught her attention.

So, she took it from the musician, tuned it a bit, and began to play. A miniature silver sphere appeared next to her guitar, amplifying its sound that could be heard well throughout Heliopolis. People loved the fact that she was so versatile, that she could also play an instrument. And not only did she play it, she played it masterfully! Judging by her technique, ease, and confidence, it was apparent that she was an experienced musician. The instrument seemed completely in her control, without secrets left for her to uncover. Her playing looked so effortless and simple, like a flowing creek or a group of playing children. Her fingers were all over the strings, like a myriad of rain droplets on a smooth surface. Then, while playing, she started to sing. It was a well-known song about Heliopolis, but her interpretation and angelic voice gave it a completely new dimension. Her music blended with all there was inside the city, connecting its parts and people, into a beautiful, harmonious union. The spirit of her sound touched people deeply, vibrating and flowing through them, creating in everyone a desire to join their voices with hers. A second or so later, and everyone was singing. What an incredible experience!

"What can I say..." Nel, somewhere in the audience, said to Niskala. "She is the next wonder of the world."

"Look at my arm. Goosebumps!" Said Niskala.

After her performance, as visitors were approaching Adiana to greet her, she hugged everyone and warmly smiled at them. When they left, Niskala approached and gave her a huge hug.

"On Saturday," Adiana said to her "my parents will have a feast, and we would very much like if you and your family could join us. They are so excited to meet you. Can you come?"

"Of course, we will! How exciting!" beamed Niskala. "I'll have to be a bit late since a new pyramid is being erected on the same day, and I have to be present. But, Nel and the kids will come on time." She turned towards Nel and asked, "Can you go, dear?"

"Certainly. We'll be there. With reinforcement. Icarus will come too. He's practically family, as you know," Nel added. He sensed that Niskala wanted to be with Adiana alone, so he greeted them, and took the children elsewhere.

"I had no idea you could play guitar so well," Niskala said to Adiana. "How long will you continue to surprise us, I wonder?" Niskala said smiling.

"Oh that," Adiana laughed. "We should thank my father for that. He is a musician. But he never forced instruments on me as an obligation. When he saw that I was constantly around them, trying to play, he pulled some strings, and he and his friends taught me," Adiana explained.

"Oh my goodness. Instruments? Plural? I can already see that you all will have a great time without me on Saturday," Niskala said with a sad face that quickly turned to a smile. "But no worries, I'll join you as soon as possible."

"Of course. Can't wait for you to meet my parents," Adiana said, as she hugged her again.

"I have something for you," Niskala said. "A small token of appreciation for bringing joy to people's lives with your storytelling." Niskala took off her necklace with the Sun pendant spreading its rays. On the rays were miniature spheres, next to each other. Then she put the necklace around Adiana's neck.

"Oh, how beautiful it is. Thank you, Niskala. I'll always treasure it." She wiped her teary eyes. "I already know what gift I'll give you," Adiana said.

"*You* are my best present, Adiana. And everyone else's. You are our treasure," Niskala said, wiping tears from Adiana's face.

CHAPTER SEVEN

DARKNESS IN THE WAY OF LIGHT

Nel, the children, and Icarus went to meet Adiana's family and enjoy the feast, while Niskala attended the opening of a new pyramid in Heliopolis. That same day, the pyramid was supposed to be ready for visitors so that they could enjoy the full experience of its purpose—teaching people to be able to control their emotions. The pyramid was supposed to be 50 meters high, like all pyramids in Heliopolis, and it would have an internal wall, featuring video projections. The pyramid would also contain another inner wall that would be made into a massive art piece. Just like the rest of Heliopolis's pyramids, this one too would contain, in its center, several smaller pyramids, each 50 square meters. Thus, the idea was to erect a complex, a tall building, so it was natural to ask how to create such a structure in only one day. The answer: Utilize the technology of skalium-made spheres. What were these spherical entities?

In the past, a team of researchers, led by Niskala, managed to produce a material that they named skalium. It was designed to assume the shape and composition of any matter. Skalium spheres were made of such a material that when Niskala issued a command, the spheres connected with each other in a network, and managed to construct anything they were asked to. Almost instantaneously, the spheres could transform into water, titanium, mercury, gold, air, fire, earth, and so on. Children, especially, liked when Niskala instructed a sphere to lift off her palm and become a dandelion. She would blow into it, dispersing its seeds. They would then transform into soap bubbles, and children would run after them, catching, poking, and blowing them away. To children, it looked like magic, but it was actually an advanced science. The entirety of Heliopolis was made from these spheres in only one day, so creating a pyramid in a single day, with such advanced technology, was a relatively simple task to complete.

In Heliopolis, where a new pyramid was about to arise at any moment, Niskala stood holding a sphere in her palm. A lot of people were about to witness the upcoming spectacle. She ran her finger over the sphere's surface, typed something in it, a code. The object detached from her palm and flew to the location where the pyramid was supposed to materialize. Suddenly, many more spheres detached from the walls of Heliopolis very quickly, as if they were released arrows, joining the single sphere, levitating in the center of the pyramid to be. Skalium walls, that seconds ago gave birth to the spheres, regenerated completely, without leaving any trace of a missing sphere, as if nothing had happened there. Spheres began connecting with one another, and the foundation of the pyramid, as well as its sides, grew quickly. In under a minute, the pyramid was complete. Silver spheres that created it became white, and one white side of the pyramid became transparent glass—the pyramid's entrance. As Niskala approached the entrance, the glass material thinned, and finally completely vanished before her. After the people who followed her entered the pyramid, the glass entrance rematerialized.

Inside the pyramid, along its tall, left-side wall, projections of soothing landscapes were visible: A blue sky above a desert, where the wind was scattering sand from the dunes; a caravan of camels slowly moving through the sand; a tropical island with palm leaves and branches moving in the wind; subtle waves, reaching the island's shore with scattered sea-shells of various colors; moonlight flickering on the surface of a lake; a man working in a zen garden, creating shapes in the sand with a rake; flight through clouds in the sky. The pyramid's right wall was made up of a tall stained-glass window, depicting the symbol of Heliopolis—the sun emanating eight unstoppable rays passing through a circle, containing the sun in its center. Dominating colors in the stained-glass artwork were yellow, orange, and blue, and joy and tranquility would descend upon an observing person.

The pyramid's floor was white and smooth, with white leather sofas here and there. Next to each sofa was a tree, and a coffee table with snacks and drinks. In the middle of the pyramid were smaller ones, each as tall as a two-storey building. Niskala approached one of the pyramids, and addressed the visitors:

"This new pyramid...," she said pointing to the entire interior, "... will help us control our emotions. Here, we will learn to reduce the negative ones, replacing them with the positive. Also, you will learn what to do to maintain positive emotions, and to amplify them. I'm here for the first time, just like you, and, like you, I'm very excited to see what the teachers prepared for us today." She paused for a few seconds and added: "We have four pyramids here, each one has the same theme, but since there are a lot of you today, some of you will need to wait your turns. But, don't worry, there are quite enough sofas and armchairs around, so you can just sit here, and enjoy the wait. Heliopolis randomly creates a list of who goes first and who follows, so when you see your photograph on the wall of this pyramid..." she pointed to the one next to her, displaying her photograph as an example, "...that means it's your turn to enter."

As she was talking, Niskala spotted a woman, dressed all in black, with a hood hiding her face. It was a rather unusual sight since nobody else was dressed like that. Then, something even stranger happened. The woman was in one location, and then suddenly appeared in a different, distant spot. The woman did not walk—she just disappeared and reappeared again in another location. Shortly, the woman repeated this strange behavior one more time. Niskala registered the phenomenon immediately, very much surprised by what she saw, expecting that the woman would approach her soon.

It seemed she wanted to attract Niskala's attention, to let her know that she was not ordinary at all. Soon, Niskala suspected, the woman would reveal her intentions.

Four other people and Niskala entered the small pyramid and proceeded to sit at the glowing, oval table in the middle of the room. The left-side wall had projections like in the outside pyramid, and the right-hand wall was a smaller replica of the stained glass window from the outside. Everyone was delighted that Niskala was among them, and they exchanged a few cordial words with her. Across the table from them was a female teacher, smiling enthusiastically about the workshop she had prepared. A woman who was sitting to Niskala's immediate left whispered to Niskala that she did not feel that well, that she suddenly had an intense headache, was nauseated, and had to leave. Niskala hugged her, concerned for her well-being, and wished her a fast recovery without making anything more out of it. Niskala felt a sudden, sharp drop in temperature to her left. In the chair next to her was the hooded woman in black. She must have appeared out of nowhere, Niskala thought, since she did not hear anyone approaching. The woman just sat motionlessly, looking straight ahead, without turning her head or making any contact with Niskala, who could only see her profile shrouded in mystery by the hood.

"Your family is at the feast with Adiana and her parents..." The woman in black spoke.

"Yes?" Niskala said, surprised.

"When I leave this room, you have five minutes to surrender the technology of skalium spheres to me. I will be in the tower outside this pyramid. If you disobey, your family, Adiana and her family will be dead." When Niskala heard this, she turned pale.

Still looking straight ahead, without making contact with Niskala, the woman in black continued: "For seven days they will be possessed by demons, who will suppress their personalities and torture their bodies. Your loved ones will attack others and injure themselves by pulling out their hair, eating rocks and glass, breaking their nails scratching the walls. Their voices will be silenced, and demons will speak through them. On the seventh day, they will die after suffering from excruciating hunger and thirst, yet the demons will not allow them to eat or drink." The woman spoke these words without moving.

"Through centuries..." she continued, "the process has been perfected. There is no cure. The destiny of those you love is in your hands," she warned and then disappeared.

Shocked, with a knot in her stomach, Niskala remained in her seat, as if she had turned to stone. She knew that this was neither a joke nor a bluffing. The woman was not human. She was a demon. Niskala knew that she had to regain composure, that she could not allow panic to overpower her. In this situation, anyone would be overwhelmed with a myriad of thoughts and feelings, a thorny ball of confusion, fear, and helplessness. The internal conflict would tear anyone apart. Should she surrender the mighty technology to a person who could destroy the world with it, or not surrender it and lose family and friends, instead? Thinking along those lines would result in feelings of guilt regardless of which option she chose. But, Niskala would not be Niskala if she allowed herself such self-harming reflections; instead, she worked on remaining calm, on being rational such that she could soon reverse the situation to her advantage.

Without thinking of anything else, she focused on applying what she already knew about controlling one's emotions. First, breathing. She inhaled deeply and slowly to relax herself as much as possible. With a finger she covered one of her nostrils, deeply inhaling through the other one; then she moved her finger over the other nostril, inhaling a deep breath through the open one. This ancient Pranayama technique stimulated both brain hemispheres with oxygen, allowing her entire brain to function better. She concentrated on something positive in this situation, thinking encouraging thoughts: "You are alive and well, like the rest of the people you love. Turn the situation to your advantage by using reason. You will prevail, as you always do!"

Niskala didn't say much to anyone; she just smiled at the instructor and told her that she had to leave due to some other obligations. Niskala didn't increase her pace; she just walked towards the tower, slowly, so she could save energy and remain calm. She also didn't want to attract attention and cause concern for others. Making eye contact with the people and children, who were passing by, and smiling at them, being typical Niskala, nobody suspected anything.

Focusing on the beauties of Heliopolis, Niskala prevented gloomy thoughts from consuming her. Feelings of being in control are empowering at moments like these, Niskala knew that; thus, she became aware that the demon depended on her cooperation. It was irrelevant whether that was truly the case, but what mattered was that Niskala genuinely felt that way. Controlling one's emotions also includes recalling the cause of the negative feelings, and interpreting them in a way that does not sustain the negative emotion any longer; hence, Niskala thought of the woman in black as having the potential for becoming a good person.

Niskala entered the tower... In a dimly lit environment, she made out barely-noticeable, vertically elongated, tinted windows, receiving minimal light from Heliopolis. The dark interior of the tower was well-known to her, so the poor visibility did not present an obstacle. The upper level, which could be reached with wings, became illuminated at a particular time only—the time of a beautiful ceremony, marking one's transformation into a better person. Niskala was focusing her attention on those positive memories.

From the tower's entrance, a corridor of pedestals stretched towards the wall opposite the entrance. On each pedestal was a pair of wings. Niskala could not see anyone in the room, yet she sensed a sudden decrease in temperature, and in it, someone's presence. She sensed that she was being observed. Coldness was coming from the point where the pedestals ended, close to the wall. Niskala stepped into the corridor, approaching the epicenter of coldness.

She saw a shadow on the wall, resembling a human-like figure. From the pedestal closest to that wall, a pair of wings collapsed to the floor, as if someone or something forcefully pushed them with the intent to intimidate and frighten Niskala. But, she didn't even blink; there was no fear in her, only clarity of mind, awareness of the present moment, and calmness. Suddenly, the two-dimensional shadow on the wall evaporated, and from it materialized the hooded woman in black, standing next to the empty pedestal, facing Niskala.

The woman placed something small, moving and alive on the pedestal. Niskala saw contours of a tiny creature and its eyes. It was a kitten. It came closer to the pedestal's rim, estimating whether it could jump to the floor; it then stepped back and meowed, looking at the woman, then at Niskala, as if asking for help. As Niskala made a step towards the kitten, the surge of freezing coldness pushed her back, signaling her to stop. A spherical vessel appeared from nowhere in the woman's hand... She dipped the tips of her fingers into it, moving them to the kitten's mouth. The kitten licked them, and the spirit of wildness possessed it... it hissed, growled, arched its back, with fur standing on edge. It was ready to strike, making fast, abrupt scratching movements towards Niskala. It twisted and turned its limbs, and bit itself, causing bleeding on its shaking body. Then, it dropped dead. Still, Niskala did not flinch, realizing that the woman was trying to throw Niskala off her mental balance with fear and intimidation. This was a demonstration of power, Niskala knew, with bizarre symbolism, where the kitten represented the innocent ones that Niskala loved. This was a reminder and warning about what would happen to them if Niskala did not obey.

"I like your outfit," Niskala complimented. "Perhaps I should start wearing black too. It would make me look thinner." She introduced an element of humor, to maintain the continuity of her positive thoughts and feelings. Then, she visualized Nel, Icarus, Io, Nora, and Adiana, all smiling and having a good time. She thought about how they hugged her, knowing that the support of her loved ones was very important in times of crisis like this. The woman in black extended her empty palm to Niskala, and demanded:

"The sphere."

Niskala addressed the wall in a different language: "Saluma, onofre te mae pala," and a sphere detached from the wall, landing on her palm. Then, without hesitation, she placed the sphere onto the woman's palm.

"Explain how to use it," the woman demanded.

Niskala ran her finger over the sphere, drawing an image of concentric circles, and a file appeared on the surface. She touched it with her finger, and the sphere projected a holographic image with categories: Commands by touch, speech, body movements. Niskala pressed the "commands by touch" category, and the hologram of an instructor began explaining how to use the sphere.

"Show me how to speed up the instructions," the woman commanded.

"With your finger, write 5505 on the surface. All instructions will be compressed into 30 seconds." As Niskala said it, the woman imported the code. The woman did not move, intensely focusing on the instructions that rapidly unfolded. It appeared she was learning, memorizing. Then, the woman typed a code on the sphere, and it turned off. She opened her mouth, and thick, wavy smoke came out of her mouth, materializing in human-like forms, all clothed in black, with hoods. Twenty demons surrounded Niskala, and she began shaking due to the waves of freezing coldness.

"What is the weakness of the spheres?" a male voice asked.

"The only weakness," said Niskala, shaking from coldness "is that the system does not have a moral code. In my hands, the spheres do good deeds, in evil hands, they can be used for wrongdoings." She could dwell on the regret she felt for not installing the moral values into the system, but she did not burden herself with that—there was no use. Everything that was negative, feelings of guilt especially, did not help her now. Any negativity would disturb her inner peace.

"Saluma, onofre te mae pala," the woman in black said, and another sphere detached from the wall, landing on her palm. She handed it to Niskala, who, without any questions, took it. She didn't ask why she was holding the sphere; she did not let confusion plague her mind. She just accepted this mysterious gesture.

"You will demonstrate how the system operates. On a real life example," the woman said, and as she finished her command, all of the demons, including her, disappeared. All the wings from the pedestals collapsed on the floor. The coldness in the room vanished. Niskala knew that she did not have a lot of time, that the demons would be back, so she picked up the first pair of wings from the floor and put them on. Moments later, in all Heliopolises throughout the planet, on all walls where the projections were occurring, a news anchor addressed the visitors:

"Dear visitors, I am sorry to ruin your enjoyment of Heliopolis, but a tsunami is heading towards the populated islands in the Lacrimal Sea. The lives of 200,000 people are in serious danger. Please stay tuned, since your help may be needed. For now, just send your positive thoughts to those who are in danger. We will pray for their lives."

Niskala was the only one who knew that the tsunami was a demonic deed, that it was created by the spheres. She flew up to a higher level of the tower, which had a balcony attached to it. From there she could see the entire interior of Heliopolis. She typed a code in her sphere, and her image was on all the walls of every single Heliopolis.

"Dear friends, I had to build Heliopolis in one day, and years of solving problems have prepared me for what awaits us. In other words, this unfolding crisis is not foreign to me. As you know from stories, I was in numerous difficult situations, but every single time, I came out stronger and wiser. This time will be no different. I am only asking you for patience, and hope that everything will soon be back to normal."

She typed a code on the sphere's surface, and the ceiling of Heliopolis opened, letting her fly towards the clouds. Thousands of spheres detached from the walls of Heliopolis, following her. The loyalty of her skalium fleet sparked additional courage and strength in Niskala.

CHAPTER EIGHT

A SUDDEN TURN

Niskala was flying over the serene side of the Lacrimal Sea. The surface was smooth like glass, and the water was crystal clear, so much so that her gaze reached the sea's floor, with long traces of starfish in the sand, touched by the delicate rays of the sunlight. Flying over the populated islands, she saw migrations of people, moving rapidly from the lower altitudes to the higher ones, trying to survive the wave's impact. Helicopters could be seen too, attempting to board as many people as possible. She was approaching the wild side of the sea. In the distance, above the rough sea, she saw thunderbolts, tornadoes, and dark clouds--recognizable features of the sea's terrifying power--getting closer and closer to her.

Niskala held her sphere, getting ready to call Nel, but she hesitated. What would she even tell him about the entire situation without the line being disconnected by the demons? From the moment she surrendered the technology of spheres, the governing of the planet was in demonic hands. Their power was limitless now. With her skalium spheres they could control anything, and have insight into all aspects of human society. Niskala decided to make a call anyway; she touched the sphere with her finger, and the sphere split into two smaller ones; one came close to her mouth, and the other landed nearby her ear. When he was on the line, she said,

"Nel, my love. I am so glad to hear your voice. How are the kids?"

"Everyone is just fine, dear. Don't worry. How are you? You must be getting ready to confront the tsunami."

"That's right," she said. "I am doing fine, but I wanted to tell you that the problem is more complicated."

"Tsunami? What's that for the great Niskala, the heroine forged in hundreds of adventures? Go get it, tigress!"

Niskala laughed a little and continued, "It is not only the tsunami; just know that I will always love you. Goodbye for now; I need to face this," she explained.

"I wish you lots of luck! Full throttle, love! But know that you will not be facing the wave alone," Nel reassured.

"What do you mean?" Niskala asked.

"Turn around," he prompted.

When she turned around, she saw something she couldn't believe. With his wings spread, Nel was piercing through the mist of the clouds, coming closer to her. A surge of joy overwhelmed her. She wiped her happy tears, spreading her arms towards him. A second or two later, and they were connected in the clouds, firmly hugging, and passionately kissing.

She typed something on the sphere, and hundreds of them flying nearby, including the ones that came with Nel, flew far away from them. "That should take care of anyone being able to eavesdrop on our conversation," she explained, whispering in his ear:

"I had to surrender the spheres to demonic beings. If I didn't, many people I love would be dead by now."

"What do they want?" Nel whispered.

"I can't predict their next move, but I know that they used spheres to engineer the tsunami. By observing how I deal with it, they are learning about the spheres' capabilities as we speak."

"Let's not worry about demons right now. They aren't stronger than our love!" Nel said, reassuring her. Niskala drew an object in the air calling several spheres to her. On one of them she typed a code, and the spheres connected, transforming into a pair of binoculars. Through it, she saw the tsunami looming in the distance.

"Our love and friendship," she added, looking through the binoculars, "amazes me." She handed the binoculars to Nel, shaking her head in disbelief, with a big smile on her face. Their friend Icarus was surfing down the tsunami, on a surfboard. When he reached the bottom of the wave, his wings unfolded, lifting him up above the top of the wave, letting him hover there. Before the surfboard hit the surface of the sea, it broke down into many spheres that quickly reassembled into the surfboard right below Icarus's feet. He went down one more time.

Nel laughed. "Yep! A man one can always count on. The one and only Icarus! A creator, an artist, a scientist, an adventurer. Above all that, my brother from another mother. Great, fearless Icarus."

Niskala drew a shape in the air, a code, and another sphere flew back towards her. She typed a code on the dial pad of its surface, and the sphere divided in two smaller spheres becoming her phone. She moved the spheres close to Nel's head.

"How are you big boy?" Nel said talking into the sphere.

"Ecstatic, euphoric, never better!" Icarus responded, speaking into a sphere close to his mouth. One more time he surfed down the wave, with his hand raised high up in the air, clenching it into a fist, greeting his friends.

"For friendship and humanity!" he exclaimed. Then he flew off the wave towards Nel and Niskala, followed by many spheres that accompanied him. In a few more seconds, he was next to them.

"Well, my friends, we waited for a long time for a new adventure. This is our chance to refresh our memories about what we can do as a team," Icarus said enthusiastically.

"Ok boys, this is the plan," Niskala took charge. "The tsunami is 3 kilometers wide. I will go in the middle, Nel goes left, Icarus right. We will fly above the sea's surface forming a line, and when I give a sign, each one of us will deposit one sphere into the sea." She was typing codes on three spheres and handed one to Icarus, the other one to Nel. One remained with her.

"When you deposit them into the water, the spheres will know what to do next—they'll build a barrier. Do you like my plan, or can you think of something else?" she asked.

"The plan is good," Icarus exclaimed, "But, don't spheres know what to do even without us? You can program them with the code, right?"

"I sure can," she reassured them. "But, then, what would the two of you do? What exactly would your roles be here?" she laughed, and Icarus and Nel did too. Niskala continued: "Since both of you wish to be a part of a new adventure so much, this is your chance to get involved. Plus, it would be wonderful to do this together, wouldn't it? For old time's sake?" They all agreed.

"Modern technology replaces the human factor and takes away the allure of adventures. But, we are happy to participate even in some small way," Icarus said.

"True," Nel agreed.

"Ok, just follow me. We need to remain in the same line. Nel goes left, Icarus right, and I go in the middle," Niskala clarified one last time, and then she flew towards the rough sea, flying above the surface. The tsunami was rapidly approaching. She stopped, hovering above the surface, and deposited her sphere into the sea. The tsunami could still be seen in the distance, and it was moving fast. Three minutes to collision with the first island. Nel went far left from Niskala, parallel to the tsunami. Icarus went right, assuming the same position. The three of them were like three dots on a single horizontal line. Nel and Icarus dropped their spheres into the sea, and instantly, all spheres that came with them from Heliopolis, thousands of them, dived into the sea following the three initial spheres. Under the surface, spheres were rapidly connecting, building a gigantic wall. In a matter of seconds, a formidable, metal wall started to rise from the sea. It was as high and wide as the tsunami, and it stood firmly waiting. 60 more seconds to impact...40...15...5... and collision.

The thundering sound of the impact was overpowering, and the tsunami pushed the wall for an entire kilometer. But, the giant wave was stopped. Hovering above the wall's top, Nel, Niskala, and Icarus gestured high-fives to one another. They looked into the serene side of the sea, where the islands were. If the wall had not held the tsunami, many lives would have been lost. Niskala typed something on a sphere, and several spheres connected, creating three cold bottles of a refreshing drink. Each of them took one and drank. They had no idea what was to come next...

"Like good ol' times," Icarus said, "when we lived for adventures on Heaven and Earth." And he clinked his bottle against Nel's and Niskala's.

"Hear, hear!" Niskala agreed. "As above, so below," she added.

"Long live adventures, and to our being together in them," Nel added.

"Well, guys, I am delighted that you were able to revisit the days when you were younger, thinner, and had better reflexes," Niskala said teasing them.

"Hey, hey, old lady..." Nel was about to finish his joke, but then something happened that contradicted common sense. Something unreal. Impossible. Horrible. The wall they were sitting on just exploded, as if someone detonated it. Huge pieces of metal were catapulted in all directions, like grenade shrapnel, piercing everything in their way, falling into the sea, whistling through the air, as if there were a heavy bombardment. In a split second, Niskala, Nel, and Icarus were wiped off the wall, hit by pieces of flying metal, and they fell into the sea.

Nel, bleeding from many wounds, opened his eyes. He was lying on his wings, alone in the rough sea, with no one around, only waves and sky with thundering bolts of lightning. Away from him he spotted Niskala's bloody wings floating on the surface. At first, he thought this was a horrible dream, a nightmare, from which he would soon wake up. Surely this couldn't be. Then, panic overwhelmed him. Where was his Niskala?

"Niskala! Niskala!" He yelled as loudly as he could, but... He swam here and there, in circles, fighting with the waves, looking for her, but she wasn't there. He reached her wings, hoping that she was holding them, but she wasn't. Only her wings remained, covered in blood. He looked under the water, but it was too dark to see. He was calling her, and calling, yelling and yelling, but no response. Then, panic gave way to despair. He began to realize that she was gone. That she wasn't coming back. He saw Icarus's body with the back of his head turned towards the sky, his face facing in the sea. He turned Icarus's body over, trying to feel a pulse on his neck, but it was pointless. He looked at his own wounds, at how much blood he was losing... He would not last much longer, he realized. His heavy eyelids were stronger than his desire to remain awake, to keep looking. They closed, firmly. And did not open again.

...

Niskala was dead.

Her body, riddled with countless wounds, was sinking in the sea, leaving behind a bloody trail. Soon, her body touched the sand. Peace and darkness, like a shroud, covered her.

What an immeasurable tragedy.

Words do not exist to accurately depict how the news about Niskala's death devastated people. Everywhere, thick, impenetrable darkness enveloped the human soul. Wherever people were, regardless of the time of the day, night fell upon them. No death of any leader ever affected the human race this much, since she was the only one in history who managed to transform human beings into people who radiated virtues. No one had ever accomplished anything as profound and magnificent as Niskala had. From a lost species, moving steadily towards self-destruction, she preserved the best of it, and from mere potential for a better existence, she chiseled a higher, enlightened human being who enriched reality with its inspiring life. Everyone knew what Niskala had achieved, and they loved her dearly for what she had done for the world. They loved her for her virtues: Humility, fairness, bravery, persistence, patience, compassion, and forgiveness, to name just a few of her admirable traits.

There is a story that captures these beloved aspects of Niskala. Years ago, when Nel realized that the Lacrimal Sea, his creator, could be able to reveal to him what happened to his old self, why he lost his soul, and how to reclaim it, he flew to the sea. At its shores, he met Io, a boy, around five years old, who suddenly appeared on the horizon, sailing in a boat by himself. After several days of spending time with Io, playing, riding in the boat, fishing and cooking, Niskala showed up on the doorstep of the cabin where Nel and Io stayed.

"I received your message," she said, hugging Nel, with sadness and concern in her eyes. "I'm very sorry that you cannot come back with us to Solaris." She hugged the little boy whom she saw for the first time.

"I am very sorry too, Niskala, but I must go my own way," responded Nel.

"Wait," she said, "do you feel better here?"

"Yes, I do. The sea and Io have a positive effect on me, but that's not enough. I know the way... The sea has revealed it to me."

"What's your plan? Can you share it with me?" Niskala asked.

"It's to seek out the conflict between good and evil. Only that can return my soul. I will, of course, be on the side of goodness," Nel clarified.

"But, we already have a better future. Didn't we fight for it? Didn't you already die once for it?"

"I know, but this new world, your world, Niskala, is killing me. I belong to the old world. I can't adjust to peace and progress. My soul wasn't made for this world. It was forged in the old one. I need that world back."

"Let's try together to decipher what the sea has shown you. Perhaps you made a mistake. That can happen to anyone. Perhaps someone wiser than we are can help," she implored.

"Niskala," Nel gently touched her arm, "really, there is no need. Thank you, I appreciate your wish to help, I really do, but I know what the sea showed me."

"Just, please, listen to me." Niskala was not giving up. "Io did not show up in your life exactly at this time, here, in vain, or by coincidence. The sea is trying to tell you something... Instead of searching for your salvation outside of yourself, find it within. The illness you have, the loss of your identity, the disappearance of your soul, it is a desperate call of your inner child to discover it—it needs you, it feels lost, you need to find it, it is in you, somewhere, deep down. Connect with it, and the child will free you from the need for conflict between good and evil."

"That inner child, Niskala, it doesn't exist in me any longer. The wheel of history took it away, and keeps it imprisoned where my soul is," Nel said.

"It's still in here," she put her hand on his chest. "The child is still deep inside. I can feel it. And it will heal you from that need to fight. You just need to find it... by being curious, through attempts to create, by protecting yourself from everything negative and by exposing yourself to the positive side of life. Through letting us care for you and love you. It's a process, and it will take time, but it will be worth it in the end, you will see," she said.

"The child is gone, Niskala. The old world took it away from me. I may rediscover it in me but only after I retrieve my old soul. The path ahead of me is very different, the opposite of the one you recommend."

"I'll be with you every step of the way. We'll find it in you. I know we will. Please stay. Give us a chance," she pleaded. But, he had already made up his mind.

"Thank you, Niskala. I know I can always rely on you. But, I must take the road I feel is the correct one. This time alone," he said.

"Ok, I understand." She was visibly disappointed. "I wish you luck and know that you'll always be in our hearts and minds. If you ever need me, I'll always be available for you. I love you." She looked into his eyes, but he diverted his gaze. He did not love her anymore, and she knew it.

"I'll think of you too. I hope we'll meet again soon and fly again together." He bent to tie Io's shoelace, gently touched the boy's head, hugged Niskala, and left the cabin.

"Don't you want to take your wings with you?" Niskala asked. "They can be very useful. There will be obstacles on the path you chose."

"No, Niskala. We, who search for war, we're already fallen. We don't deserve wings. We'd pollute the sky," he said, and he left to board Io's boat.

If, however, he had listened to her advice, if he had been willing to try it, he would have avoided the many years of pointless and dangerous wanderings. In the end, he realized that Niskala was right. He was fortunate enough to avoid his destruction, discovering his inner child who purified him from his irrational needs. In fact, his inner child reached for Nel, from the depth of his being, when he became a prisoner of terrifying dreams, the kind of dreams from which one does not wake up—nightmares, like black holes, sucking him in without letting his light escape. His child, innocent, playful, with no knowledge of evil, pulled him out of destruction, to his awakening, beyond the need for war, beyond the wheel of history. Niskala found him in a distant land, Dreamland, the only vestige of the old world, of the past, of human history. She nursed him back to his full recovery, loving him all the way, without reservations.

That's who Niskala was: Resilient, forgiving, patient, compassionate, made of hope and love, wise. She kept loving those who did not love her any longer, knowing that everyone has a seed of love within, that tiny quantum of potential energy to love, which can mature, grow and manifest in reality. She firmly believed that the human race could be different, better, improved. Niskala focused on that aspect, on the positive, on the potential. For every problem, she eventually found a solution, sometimes sooner, sometimes later, but she always prevailed. She was a problem-solver who knew how to depart from the standard way of thinking and embrace a completely new perspective of looking at things, a novel, refreshing view suitable for the particular situation she was in. And then, she acted, successfully, in accordance with that view.

For example, in the recent human past, Niskala realized that the intensifying nightmares plaguing humanity were due to bad genes. It was important to neutralize these rogue genes; otherwise, the human race would come to an end due to a global lack of sleep. Everyone thought that Niskala's technology was capable of accomplishing this, but that turned out to be mere wishful thinking. Icarus, who was a genius for finding solutions in biology, chemistry, physics and engineering, did not have a solution for this particular problem. Other brilliant scientists were without ideas as well. No matter what interventions were attempted, the bad genes could not be dealt with successfully. Even when they were eliminated, the success was temporary, for a couple of hours only; the same genes regenerated from the DNA molecules, in front of everyone's eyes, under the microscope.

The genesis of the dark side of the human heritage was a fact laughing in Niskala's face. They could only wonder what the cause of this drive to recreate negative genes was. That particular piece of the puzzle remained an unsolved mystery. Icarus commented frequently: "Too bad that we still have so much to learn about genetics." He would repeat those same words over and over, shrugging his shoulders, anxiously pacing. But for learning, there was no more time—people were getting sicker every day from sleep deprivation.

Unrest was expanding, deepening. Niskala did not sleep any longer either, not due to nightmares, she was immune to them, but due to a sense of responsibility, an obligation to save humanity from its imminent demise. But, not even once did she doubt that the solution existed, even though she did not know the path to it. So, although she had faith, a surprisingly unwavering one, she could not see the way. Not yet at least... To make things worse and less hopeful for others, even the Lacrimal Sea was without an answer this time. When Niskala went there to ask for help, the only thing she received from it was a message in a bottle—in its water, there was a seahorse, wrapped around a piece of coral, creating with its twisted body the shape of a question mark. Everyone lost hope after the Lacrimal Sea's inability to help; it was the final blow, but not for Niskala. She never gave up, and everyone wondered where her unbreakable will came from. In those moments people realized that hope was fundamental to her being, the source of her existence.

"Perhaps the path to a solution lies in a complete change of our approach to finding it," she suggested one morning. "We haven't tried one last thing." People were silent and held their breath as they waited to hear more about what was on Niskala's mind.

"What we can do, is to do nothing at all," she explained. "I would like an entire day to do exactly that--nothing. Just to exist in the present moment and absorb nature, its beauty, its scents, and the light of the sun."

So, she took her wings and flew to an island that was a good place to rest her body and mind. She landed on a road of tiny pebbles, covered here and there with pinecones and tiny branches. On one side of the road were pine trees, white rocks, and the calm sea. On the other side were pine trees, lavender, rosemary, and jasmine flowers covering a hill populated with small, scattered houses. She ran her fingers through the flowers, bringing them closer to her nose, taking in their intoxicating scents.

Those scents and sights, the caresses of flowers and sounds of crickets, had a very calming effect on her mind, and she was soothed further by the sound of tiny waves gently lapping against the rocks. She took a pinecone and deeply inhaled its scent... it had a mixture of sea, pine trees, fresh resin, unburdened childhood, innocence, and happiness. She heard seagulls in the distance, and, through the pine tree branches, she saw scattered sunlight on the sea's surface, where dolphins were jumping, following a couple of sailboats passing by in slow motion.

All that together altered her consciousness, unlocking a gate into an existence in the present moment. She had no recollections of the past any longer, and she had no thoughts of the future. Only here and now existed for her, and she felt oneness with nature, with its simplicity and hospitality. All of her worries suddenly left her, making her feel liberated and rejuvenated. That particular state of mind helped her see the birth of Heliopolis in a game that children played on that very same road.

Niskala always consulted with others regarding important decisions since she believed in teamwork, in togetherness. The reason nature is so magnificent, miraculous is because it does not work alone in isolation, but through the harmony of its components—Niskala used to say. That's one of the reasons why her castle was not only hers, but she shared it with many families who made their home there. Joy, optimism and hope shone from her, and the smile on her face rarely left. Seeing her during a rainy day meant seeing the shining sun in the midst of gloominess. She was a positive change in everyone's life. And many other wonderful things could be said about her. For being so special, she was a part of everyone's family. Her departure, thus, was something inconceivable, unimaginable, contrary to the rules of logic, unreal. And now this… Her abrupt death.

Days after she was gone, everyone was crushed, lost. Tears poured down the people's faces; they felt abandoned, and they stopped in their development. People were utterly confused, in disbelief. A huge emptiness echoed through everyone's souls. In the morning, waking up felt like punishment since they had to confront the pain and reality of Niskala's absence. What now? Where to go? What direction to take? What does the next day bring? Everyone asked these questions. For difficult questions, she usually had an answer, but now life had to continue without her. And without answers. Only the uncertainty was unavoidable, unmistakable. On top of that, there was the loss of Nel and Icarus. They were also beloved, and their losses amplified the sorrow of losing Niskala.

The demonic hand that orchestrated Niskala's assassination hid the truth of what really happened. There was a major cover-up. The fact that the tsunami was made of spheres and that there was an intentional detonation of the wall were never mentioned. In every single Heliopolis, like anywhere else on the planet, the news reported only that the tsunami hit the wall, that it exploded due to the impact, and that pieces of the shattered metal hit Niskala, Icarus, and Nel, taking their lives. They were proclaimed heroes, who sacrificed themselves for humanity. Their funeral was the most visited in history, and that was that. The demonic force could now continue to fulfill its hidden agenda...

CHAPTER NINE

THE VOICE

For weeks Adiana was crushed, so much so that she could not leave her bed. It was as if she were nailed to it. Her desperate parents, partly due to the condition of their daughter, and in part to what happened to Niskala, Icarus, and Nel, kept bringing her food and drink, in very small amounts, just so she could survive. But she could not put anything in her mouth. She lost so much weight, all her strength and her beauty vanished. Once a day, she somehow managed to gather a minimum of strength to step out of the bed and reach the adjacent room, to see Nora and Io, and ask them how they were, to gently touch their heads and kiss them. The trip back to bed was especially difficult. She could barely manage to return to it without falling, holding on to the walls, in tears and excruciating mental pain, sobbing until late into the night.

Since Niskala, Nel, and Icarus were gone, the children stayed with Adiana's family. That was the wish Niskala expressed in the event something were to happen to her and to Nel, who was like a father to them. The children were old enough to understand that they would never again see Niskala, Nel, or Icarus, an absolutely horrible, confusing, and brutal truth for such young minds to accept. For Adiana, it was extremely difficult to see Nora and Io suffer so much. Yet, she did not have enough strength to help them. She felt extremely guilty for that, but there was nothing she could do. Although she had just recently met Niskala in person, she treated Adiana as her own daughter, so Adiana saw in her a second mother. For that reason, too, this was so devastating for her.

Every single night, Adiana was tortured by the same nightmare: Niskala laying on her wings, somewhere in the roughness of the Lacrimal Sea, trying to remain on the wings, holding them. She is uttering words that cannot be heard in their entirety, due to her exhaustion, pain, the sound of waves, wind and thunder. Only bits and pieces of what she is saying are heard:

"...holy books about me... holy pictures with my face... a halo... shrines with my name...." On her chest, Niskala holds a miniature sphere, and with the last atoms of her strength she brings the sphere close to the feathers of her wings... the sphere changes shape into a feather and finds its place among other ones. Every morning Adiana woke up in tears and pain recalling Niskala's suffering in the sea. Usually dreams are easily forgotten shortly after one wakes up, but not this one; the images haunted Adiana throughout the day.

About a week later, Adiana, somehow, managed to leave the house and walk, baby step by baby step, for a few minutes outside, to breathe in some fresh air and move her weakened muscles a bit so that she did not become seriously ill. She knew she had to move as well as cope with her feelings, but nothing was motivating her to do either. There was nothing in her environment that was helping her in this situation. On the faces of other people, including her parents, she only saw despair, absence of consolation, unrest, hopelessness and helplessness—terrifying things she had never seen before. She wanted to help all of them, but she didn't know how; there was no strength or motivation for it. She withdrew into herself.

Days later she began thinking that she would feel better, and perhaps get some idea of how to help others, if she started to visit places she frequented with Niskala—places where she could easily bring pleasant memories back to her mind. She thought those memories would help. So, she visited the red poppy field where they met, and the waterfall where they sat and talked for hours about their lives and worldviews. She remembered the time when she asked

Niskala which one of the three stories were correct about how she reached the wheel of history with baby Nora in it.

"All three stories are correct, to some extent," Niskala explained. "At first, I tried to locate the wheel on my own, by clicking, but it didn't work. Then, I called the bat to help me, but it couldn't do it either. There was something about the wheel, about its structure, that could not be detected by sound. In the end, my astral projection showed me the way."

Those were bittersweet memories indeed... Adiana did not go to Heliopolis anymore since no one else was there, and that fact made her so sad, that endless desolation with only intense memories like ghosts haunting this once-glorious, thriving place that stood for a symbol of humanism, happiness and unity. She knew that people were desperate, that they were not motivated to do anything, that they rarely left their homes, unless they had to. She did not step into Heliopolis, but she would, more and more often, go around it, around its facade. She would walk for hours, circling it, touching the spheres that made its magnificent structure, wanting to touch Niskala, even if that meant only through her creation.

One morning, she gathered strength to face her solitude in the interior of Heliopolis. She stepped inside, did not see a single soul. She walked through the empty parks, touched their flowers, roses, orchids, trees' bark and branches. She touched a bird of paradise, its orange and purple petals, and a drop of dew glistening in the sun. And then she heard a voice coming from all sides, loudly and clearly:

"Adiana..."

"Niskala?" Adiana, recognizing the voice that she knew so well, asked confusedly.

"Yes, Adiana... It's me..." Adiana heard the voice coming from the entirety of Heliopolis. She could not believe what she heard, nor comprehend what was going on, or who it was. Why was she hearing Niskala's voice, and why was it addressing her. Frightened that she was losing her mind, that she was hallucinating, Adiana quickly ran out of Heliopolis.

Her parents noticed that there was something different about their daughter that day since she withdrew even more into herself, although she did eat a bit more that day, and she even smiled a couple of times—something they had not seen since Niskala's passing. During dinner, when they asked her why she was acting differently, she told them what had happened that morning in Heliopolis; she told them about the voice. She explained that she was not sure what had occurred, and that she was a bit concerned about, perhaps, losing her mind. It would not be a mistake, she suggested, that she visit a physician. But, her parents insisted that she was just fine mentally, and that she should not worry at all, that she was doing better every day. They also mentioned that those were just moments of her temporary weakness, and that all of those feelings would go away since time heals all emotional wounds. Niskala was missed by everyone, and her parents suggested that people were, due to being so fragile right now, susceptible to their minds playing tricks on them.

Adiana remained curious about the voice... She could not stop thinking about the possibility that Niskala was still alive somehow. She needed to believe and hope. So, early the next morning, she went to Heliopolis again. Just as before, she walked through the gardens, touching the flowers and trees, hoping for the same result as the day before. But, this time she did not hear anything. Very disappointed, thinking that she had just imagined the voice yesterday, she was prepared to leave Heliopolis. She was walking towards the exit, ready to leave, maybe forever, and then, she heard the voice again:

"Adiana... My dear child... Don't be afraid... It's me... Your Niskala."

When Adiana heard this, she lowered her body to the floor, lay down there, curled like a child in her mother's womb, and she started to cry uncontrollably. She cried tears of relief, disbelief, joy, hope, and confusion. Many mixed feelings overwhelmed her. Her cries echoed, bouncing through the dome.

"My dear Adiana..." The voice continued, "...I know how much my death hurts... I know it's tearing you apart... And I am so sorry that you, Nora, Io, and everyone else is going through this. But, on the bright side, I can see the world with different eyes now." Adiana managed to sit, wiping her tears, hoping to hear more.

"I found the meaning of my death, Adiana." As the voice said this, a ray of light, from above, fell upon Adiana, slowly moving to her arm and ending on her hand. Adiana opened her palm and held the ray. It was warm and gentle, like Niskala. Adiana just looked at the beam on her palm and smiled, realizing that she was establishing contact with Niskala.

"Niskala, my Niskala. Oh, how I have missed you." Adiana smiled and cried without losing the beam from her sight. Then she joined both her palms, letting the beam warm them. She slowly turned her palms as if she was washing them in that ray of light.

"I know that all of this is in my head..." Adiana said through tears, smiling, "... but it feels wonderful to be happy again, just for a moment... if only for a moment, to hear your voice that feels real."

"But, I am here with you, Adiana," the voice consoled. "On your palms, next to you, and everywhere around you."

"Where are you Niskala? Are you in this ray of light?" Adiana stared at it on her palms.

"Yes, I am. And everywhere else... in each flower, in every rock and grain in these parks here, in every tree, in windows... I am the entire Heliopolis." A myriad of light rays came out of everything in Heliopolis, and kept bathing Adiana's body and soul enclosed in the center of this gentle flood of beams. Awestruck, Adiana stood up and closed her eyes. She stretched out her arms, slowly turning them, so that she could bathe her arms and palms in the warmth of the incoming light. She moved her head slowly so that every part of her face and hair could be touched by the illuminating spirit of Niskala. Adiana deeply inhaled the moment of revelation and the scent of its sacredness.

"Now, when I see things better, there is a new mission ahead of us, my dear child," Niskala's voice said.

"What mission, Niskala? Tell me," Adiana asked curiously.

"You are chosen... by me... to assume the role I held while I was embodied in the human body, to lead the planet in the direction I led it, towards light, towards betterment. You, Adiana, and nobody else. You have wisdom and a gift of connecting with people. I hope you will accept this highest honor, and together we will make human beings even more magnificent."

"I will!" Adiana immediately agreed. "But how? How can I lead the planet? I don't know how," Adiana implored, glancing over the entire Heliopolis, looking for an answer and support.

"The election is in a few weeks... the people will choose my successor. Submit your name to be considered for taking over my role. The majority will vote for you. They already know you. They miss you. They miss your warmth, hope, and strength. When you succeed me, I will address you again. And, then, I will tell you what our next step will be. I will show you light that you have never seen or dreamed of so far," Niskala's voice exclaimed.

"Sure, Niskala. I will do as you say," Adiana assured. "How are you here? How did you survive?"

"My dear Adiana, you would not understand if I told you now. It will become clear to you once you see the light I promised you. Go now, my child and my soulmate. The entire world depends on you. Go and help the suffering souls. You are their savior now."

Full of a regenerated hope, enthusiasm, and strength, Adiana left Heliopolis. For the first time, after Niskala's death, a large smile settled on her face. Standing outside Heliopolis, Adiana looked into her reflection in the mirror-coated entrance door. She again saw her old self: Young, beautiful, radiant, full of dreams, and hopes. Her life regained its crystal-clear meaning once again.

CHAPTER TEN

THE PRIESTESS

Adiana won the election by a landslide, almost everyone voted for her. That was not a miracle at all, since she was well-known world-wide due to her charismatic personality and very impressionable and inspiring stories about Niskala, Nel, and Icarus. It is true that nobody had heard from Adiana since Niskala's death, but everyone remembered her and wished for her return. Everyone missed Niskala, but they all missed Adiana too. Obviously, people did not feel let down, but they all understood why Adiana disappeared—she was grieving like everybody else.

When people learned that Adiana was one of the candidates, that changed everything, it was as if the dark clouds were parted by a sudden sunlight. The voters saw in her a consolation for losing Niskala. Adiana reminded them of her. In addition, Adiana was the only candidate whose face was genuinely glowing; she was authentically happy; she somehow, miraculously, transcended the pain of Niskala's death. That's exactly what people needed—someone who could do just that; somebody who was strong enough to soar from a bottomless, dark pit into the blue sky.

From one debate to another, Adiana was getting better and better. While other candidates visibly struggled to find something that vaguely resembled hope and to suppress, unsuccessfully, the signs of their grief for Niskala, Adiana was totally different—with a large smile on her face and a spark in her eyes, reflecting newfound hope and happiness, instead of grief. She often referred to Niskala, as if she were still alive and well. Every quotation that she used was always in the present tense, like "Niskala teaches us," "Niskala recommends," "Niskala wishes," and so on. With Adiana talking about Niskala, people felt Niskala had not died. People loved that positive energy. They also loved the fact that nobody else but Adiana was so knowledgeable about Niskala's life; she was a fountain of accurate information about her. People saw in that an immense respect and admiration for Niskala's work, something they all now shared with Adiana.

There were other reasons why people chose Adiana. It was obvious that Niskala loved her and thought very highly of her, frequently saying that Adiana was young but wise as if she were a thousand years old. Often they were seen together, smiling, laughing, apparently enjoying each other's company. Niskala always spoke of her very highly, which was perceived as her endorsement of Adiana. Further, Adiana was young, barely twenty, and the people appreciated a certain energy of youth, a factor that would drive her to work tirelessly, like Niskala, and accomplish like deeds. Many even thought that, perhaps, Adiana would be the one who would surpass even the great Niskala.

However, nobody knew, except Adiana's parents, that she heard Niskala's voice. Adiana did not want to mention this so that others would not question her sanity. But, clearly, that same voice was the determining factor that stimulated Adiana to reconnect with her old self. That same voice was her pair of wings that pulled her out of the dark pit into the illuminated sky.

Now, Adiana had a tremendous power to lead the planet and change the world, the same power once vested in Niskala. She was offered to relocate to Niskala's castle, but before she would make her decision, she asked Nora and Io if that was something they would want. They liked that idea, since they grew up in the castle, and only for that reason Adiana agreed to move there. If it was only up to her, she would remain in her humble home. That humility and compassion towards others were just some traits that Niskala and others admired about Adiana.

The day after the election, Adiana could not wait to visit Heliopolis and tell Niskala in person about the election results. She stepped into Heliopolis and said:

"Niskala, you were right! People voted for me!"

"Congratulations, my dear one." Niskala's voice said. "I didn't doubt it, not even for a second. You deserve it! Be proud of yourself, all this is exclusively your accomplishment. I immediately recognized your inner beauty and there was nothing I would change about you," the voice added.

"Thank you so much, Niskala. When will you show me the new light? Remember that you said you would."

"Of course," the voice responded. "Let us heal people's wounds caused by my death. Let us pleasantly surprise them and fulfill the painful void in their souls with something so beautiful, so joyful, so fundamental, so pervasive, something they crave so much. Let's give them a gift of new light!"

"Yes, yes. I cannot wait, Niskala. What is the new light? What's brighter than you and Heliopolis?" Adiana asked.

For a few seconds, Niskala's voice was silent. Adiana was so excited to discover what it was all about, for she had no idea what Niskala had in mind. Then, the voice said:

"We will give to people . . . a new religion, Adiana. A religion about Holy Niskala."

When she heard that, Adiana was stunned. She had not anticipated anything like that. Details from her dreams about wounded Niskala on the wings passed through her mind, and her words when Niskala mentioned holy books about her, shrines with her name... Adiana connected those dreams with what Niskala's voice just said, and a large smile appeared on her face. It made perfect sense, so she exclaimed:

"A magnificent idea! I love it! Yes, yes! That would restore people's hopes and wishes to live. Their days would again start with something noble and beautiful: Faith in you, your teachings and your deeds. Yes! Yes! That's what we all need." Adiana could not hide her excitement.

"And you my child, you will no longer only tell stories about my life... You will have a new role, a more significant and more complex one, with much more responsibility... You will become a priestess!" The voice declared.

"A priestess? I am honored." Honored, yet confused, Adiana continued: "What am I expected to do as a priestess?"

"Nothing too different from what you have already done so far," the voice said. "You will be telling, in that mesmerizing, transcending, and unique way of yours, about me and my adventures with Nel and Icarus. From those stories you will be extracting messages, directions, of how people should live their lives. You will be revealing those messages to them. In addition, you will conduct rituals, so that all that you say is much better remembered as something sacred that touches people very deeply—the essence of their soul."

"Where will I preach your religion? In Heliopolis? Somewhere outside?" Adiana asked.

"You will build sanctuaries. Brand new ones. Soon, we will have thousands of them. All over the world. Every step of the world will be illuminated with the light of Holy Niskala. And people will forget their suffering caused by my death when I was a mere mortal. Their lives will be transformed; they will discover new meaning. They will believe again in a better tomorrow. They will believe that I am still alive, that I walk amongst them, and that I am communicating with them from an otherworldly dimension. Exactly how it is," spoke Niskala's voice.

"Yes! Yes!" Adiana exclaimed, elated. "How will I build the sanctuaries? With skalium spheres?" Adiana asked.

"Yes, dear. With the spheres. In only one day, you will be able to erect hundreds of sanctuaries. Now, you have the power, you are the supreme leader and my successor, and people chose you, so they will support your decision to build. The decoration I leave up to you in its entirety. I am sure you will do a marvelous job designing the sanctuaries, their exterior and interior," Niskala's voice explained.

"But I don't know how to use the spheres. Only you, Icarus and Nel know that," Adiana said.

"Don't worry about that. I will teach you, as I taught them. Every single secret that the spheres hide will be unveiled to you. Soon, very soon, you will be an expert in using them. You must know, however, that the skalium spheres are very powerful: they can build, but they can destroy, depending on who possesses them, right?" The voice asked.

"I know. I will not reveal the secret of using the spheres. Perhaps, only to those who become my trusted friends, like Nel and Icarus were yours," Adiana promised.

"Excellent, my dear. I know that humanity can count on you and that the planet is in good hands, in the best, as a matter of fact. Come tomorrow, at this same time, and I will show you how to use the spheres. Your training will commence," the voice said.

"Certainly, Niskala," Adiana said, and joyfully left Heliopolis.

CHAPTER ELEVEN

SPHERE BY SPHERE--SANCTUARY

The next day in Heliopolis, Niskala's voice spoke to Adiana: "Let's suppose that you want one hundred spheres to come to the center of this building. You will issue this command: 'Sekva saluma sui de tula met.' As she said these words, hundreds of spheres appeared where they were supposed to. Then the voice continued: "Sekva saluma,'" meaning "one hundred spheres." "Sui" means "fly," "de" means "in," "tula" is "the middle," and "met" means "this building."

"Sekva saluma sui de tula met," Adiana said loudly, and spheres detached from the walls, flying to the middle of the building, hovering there, awaiting the next command. This made Adiana very happy since she began understanding the language used to control the spheres. Over the next several days, she learned a lot of words and sentences in the language of the spheres. She also learned how quietly she needed to whisper so that the spheres could hear her since, in the future, it may be important to send a secretive message to them, without anyone else hearing.

She mastered commands via touch as well, drawing certain shapes and symbols on the surface of spheres. Everything that could be stated verbally, could be also expressed by touching the surface, and all that could also be done by typing certain codes onto the surface of spheres. Coded messages were a combination of digits and numbers. For example, 101R was a code commanding a sphere to start communicating with other spheres. Adiana also learned to issue a command by drawing shapes and symbols in the air with her hand, while some required both hands. The same symbols that she drew on the surface of the spheres could be drawn in the air so that the spheres could detect them from a far distance.

After a week of intensive training, Adiana learned everything that was known about spheres. She was now very familiar with the ways of commanding spheres to act, to stop whatever they were doing, to connect with other spheres in order to build objects, to establish mutual communication, and all remaining functions. The building of the sanctuaries could start. The dawn of a new religion was about to become reality.

The first sanctuary Adiana wanted to erect would be in the field of red poppy flowers, in memory of her initial meeting with Niskala. Standing in the middle of the field, holding a sphere on her palm, she imported a command. Thousands of spheres detached from the walls of Heliopolis, and in a few seconds, they were now hovering above the field. Adiana typed some additional symbols on her sphere, and very quickly the hovering spheres descended on the ground of the field, connecting with one another, rapidly building a dome, just like the one that Heliopolis had, but this one was much smaller. This one could hold up to a hundred people. While Adiana stood in the center of the building supervising the work of the spheres, the wall was quickly growing around her. Simultaneously, the circular floor underneath her feet was appearing equally fast. When the dome and the floor were completed--in just under five minutes--spheres that made up the wall and the floor, merged, and all the holes disappeared. All the surfaces were now smooth. From the outside, the dome was a polished mirror, and the inside of the dome's curved wall was made of a material resembling white glass, illuminated from within.

On the inner surface of the dome's wall, colored drawings began to appear, as if a great master depicted them fast, with such ease. The drawings reflected various scenes from Niskala's life, such as her giving the harmonica with Nel's tear inside to the horseman on the Lacrimal Sea; the sea resurrecting Nel from his tear; Niskala building bird-houses with the children in front of her castle; Niskala facing the army sitting at a table in the middle of the road; Icarus and Niskala meeting on the sand of the Lacrimal Sea; Adiana and Niskala talking face-to-face near a waterfall; Niskala stepping on large starfish that connected with one another to make a bridge from the shore to a tiny island; Nel sleeping in a tide pool in a field of many pools, Io and Niskala reaching for him, standing on the rim; Nel and Niskala hugging in the sky, wearing wings, and so on. In all the drawings, Niskala had a halo, and on the vast majority of them she smiled. Each drawing was a combination of modern, abstract art, and realism.

The floor of the sanctuary was made of a material also resembling white glass. Just like all other drawings, this one on the floor was illuminated by a light source coming from inside the glass, so that all of the details could be seen really well. In the middle of the floor was a large drawing of Niskala with her wings spread. She was hovering right above the heads of a group of children and adults. In one hand she had a skalium sphere, her arm raised towards the sky. She extended her other arm to the people below her, calling them to follow her. Her body was slightly bent since she was trying to reach them. People extended their hands towards her. She had a large smile on her face, just like the people. All were joyful about the connection that was about to happen.

The entrance into the sanctuary was based on the same mechanism from Heliopolis—as a person was coming closer to the entrance door, the spheres making up that door would gradually become air, allowing people to pass through without sensing any resistance. Then, after one would enter, the spheres would regenerate their solid state, becoming a door. Inside the sanctuary were two sets of comfortable, white armchairs, arranged as two semi-circles; one semicircle followed the curve of the left wall, and the other followed the curve of the right. There were no armchairs at the entrance or on the opposite wall. There were exactly one hundred armchairs, fifty on the left side, and fifty on the right. The area in between the armchairs, the central area, was reserved for the priestess.

"Adiana..." said the voice, when Adiana returned to Heliopolis later, "...I am completely impressed! What a magnificent sanctuary you have built for me. There are no words to express my gratitude. I, as well as the people who will be delighted by this sanctuary, thank you so much!"

"I am glad you like it, Niskala." Adiana said smiling. "I hope the others will like it too and that they will feel your presence in the sanctuary as I feel it. That is my goal."

"Absolutely! I'm sure they will. Their lost hope will be restored and rejuvenated. But, we need one more thing..." the voice spoke.

"What would that be, Niskala?" Adiana asked.

"The Holy Book," the voice responded.

"What will it be about?" Adiana was very curious.

"About the events of my life. We need a unification of my adventures and my views, so all that can be found in one place. Think of it as a holy integration in the form of a sacred text, written in a very approachable way so that everyone can understand. I will take care of that part; the spheres will take my dictation and write what needs to be written. However, I would like you to accomplish an equally important deed—designing the book. It needs to entice followers with its aura of sanctity and uniqueness."

"Such a great idea, Niskala. I am honored," Adiana said smiling, preparing to leave, so she could start working on the project of designing the book. She already had some ideas.

"One more thing, dear," the voice said before Adiana stepped out. "You will start to preach on your own, in one sanctuary, but that will be more like your initiation into the world of the priestesshood and a practice. Soon, however, we will build many more sanctuaries since people in all corners of the world need me. Other religions will, perhaps, not be enough to provide people with consolation during this transitional period when they try to adjust to the fact that I am gone. We must think of their suffering souls. Therefore, we need many priestesses like you. In every single sanctuary, a priestess just like you," the voice said.

"Like me?" Adiana was confused.

"Exactly. One Adiana per sanctuary. In every sanctuary, we need to have a priestess just like you. You will be the high priestess, their teacher and supervisor, and they will be your disciples. They will be dressed like you, with haircuts like yours, and they will learn to laugh like you, to move like you, to be you," the voice said.

"But Niskala..." Adiana did not like that idea. "... if that becomes so, we will not give those women an opportunity to be unique individuals, to be different from one another. There is only one Adiana; we don't need hundreds like me. We don't even need one more Adiana," she said.

"We do need them, Adiana; we definitely do," the voice insisted. "At the moment, you do not see reality with my eyes, but it is so important that you have faith that I can see a bit further than you. After your death, Adiana, you too will see what I am seeing since your horizon will broaden, just like it did for me. People love you, and only *you* can connect them with me. You are the bridge! Give them what they need—that ingredient of life that they are searching for. That's why they chose you for their leader. But, let me ask you something, can you be at the same place at different times?"

"No, I can't," Adiana said.

"There you go, my child. People want you, but since you cannot give yourself to everyone, you need to find those who are very similar to you. In that way people will have their Adiana in all sanctuaries--their bridge to Niskala. Establish the order of priestesses like you, choose the ones who can sing and play instruments, like you. They should look like you as much as possible. Teach them to think like you. We cannot entertain thoughts about individuality and what you are saying since our priority is to help those who suffer from losing me. We cannot abide by the principles that are important to *you*; instead, we must focus on what is important for others," the voice said. Adiana did not like what she heard, and disagreement and frustration were clearly visible on her face.

"Ha ha..." Niskala's voice laughed. "Finally! We found a tiny imperfection in you. It's about time that a wrinkle was revealed—at last. Dear, my advice has value only if it helps you become better. Nobody is perfect, as we know. I hope, in time, you will see my counsel in that light. Go now, my dearest Adiana, and don't bother yourself with this conversation. Let *me* worry about these complexities. After all, we do not need to agree about everything, do we?" the voice asked.

"I guess not. You are probably right, Niskala," Adiana said, still disappointed, since she was not on the same wavelength with Niskala regarding this. But, Adiana respected Niskala's decision, and she thought that maybe Niskala saw something that she didn't. That was the great Niskala, after all, known for her wisdom and original thinking, most likely she was right. Plus, Niskala existed in another dimension of reality; she survived death, so she probably had a better comprehension of life. Adiana left Heliopolis for the day.

CHAPTER TWELVE

DISTORTION OF TRUTH

In a few days, everything was ready, and the sanctuary was about to be opened for the visitors. There was a long line of people outside. They could not wait to get inside and hear about Niskala from Adiana, their beloved, young hope. The first group of one hundred people entered, and sat in the armchairs, enjoying how comfortable they were. The lights dimmed. Shortly, Adiana walked into the sanctuary, in a long, white robe, with her recognizable big smile. She moved into the center, above the drawing, addressing the ceiling in the language of the spheres. One detached from it and shone a beam onto her, and she was now in the pillar of light. Glancing over everyone in the room, she spoke:

"My dear ones... we have all suffered so much since the departure of our Niskala... But, today I have wonderful news for you..." She paused for a moment, with a large smile on her face, and then added: "I still hear her voice!" she exclaimed. "Louder than ever before!" She paused, seeing surprise and a bit of confusion on the people's faces. "Not in my mind, but in Heliopolis." There was a mixture of disbelief and curiosity in the room. Very quickly, that mixture turned to curiosity only.

"She still lives!" Adiana exclaimed. "Not in the same body as before, but in every single part of Heliopolis, in its every flower, in every ray of its light, in the branches, dew, windows, in every single art piece and musical note. Our grief can stop now since Niskala has returned to us; she is with us again."

Sudden calmness and smiles covered all present. Serenity removed confusion and frowns from their troubled faces. Their bodies relaxed. In that transformation, Adiana saw signs of the genesis of their faith. Yet, through the room, she felt that their faith was not yet firm, not yet strengthened and unwavering; it was still developing, in its infancy. For that faith to become stronger and enduring, she felt that they needed something... something more than just mere words. In their eyes and facial expressions, she saw a need for something real; she saw a need for Niskala's *touch*. Adiana realized that people's healing lay in that very contact; their cure was that mutual physical connection.

There was a void in the human soul, an emptiness on the material level, the plane of the physical bond with Niskala. So, at that moment, Adiana perfectly understood her role as a priestess; she was that important connection between Niskala and her people, a bridge between them, the missing link, the intermediary who makes touch happen. She walked along the armchairs, extending her palms to people, turning them up, inviting them with a gentle nod and smile to touch her. And right away the connection happened. They touched her palms, fingers, arms, and her robe. As they were doing that, tears poured down their faces, cleansing them from their grief, giving way to a solid faith in Niskala's life-force coexisting with them, manifesting through Adiana.

Adiana walked back into the center of the room. She closed her eyes for a moment. Complete silence pervaded the room.

"Our Niskala is still with us..." she said and placed her palms, one over another, tightly on her chest, as if absorbing the energy of all those touches that she collected. "She lives among us in the form of a sublime, sacred light." She lifted her palms off her chest, turning them to the people as if palms were doors that just opened, her fingers rays of light.

"She is the sacred light shining upon us from Heliopolis." As she said that, a sparkling mist of a myriad of tiny skalium spheres appeared next to her. Rapidly connecting with one another, the spheres created a rectangular shape quickly materializing into a large, thick book. In just a few seconds the book was completed, levitating next to Adiana. She took it and lifted it up above her head as the book's glow illuminated the room. The visitors were at a loss for words at how beautiful the book was.

"This is the Holy Book of Niskala. Her voice wrote it," Adiana explained. "All stories about her adventures, deeds, and wisdom are in here."

The lower half of the book cover was a mirror, the upper half transparent glass revealing the universe with stars. In the center of the book cover, was an engraved circle. In it was an image identical to the drawing on the floor underneath Adiana, except that the image in the book was a three-dimensional hologram. Looking through the circle into the image, a person would feel as if looking through a round window into the event where Niskala hovered above the people, extending her arms to them, aiming for mutual touch. The hologram looked so real, as if the contact was about to occur at any second and as if Niskala and the people would begin to speak.

Adiana carried the book through the sanctuary, holding it at the level of people's heads so they could see their reflections in it, allowing them to be a part of the impending touch with Niskala. Everyone from the audience touched the book and kissed it, without Adiana even asking. Clearly, a collective consciousness took over the sanctuary.

Adiana came to the center of the sanctuary and left the book in the air to levitate horizontally next to her. Gradually, the book's glow faded. She typed a code on the book cover, and the book opened on a certain page. For now, people could not see what was written inside since the book lay flat in the air. Adiana spoke:

"There was a time in our recent past, when darkness fell upon us. The nightmares were so intense that people were afraid to sleep. Lack of sleep led to illness, and the human race, as you recall, was about to become extinct. Today, I will remind you of the sacred event that helped Niskala realize the source of those nightmares."

She lifted the book showing the audience two pages on which the event was described. The pages were made of an opaque material, resembling white glass illuminated from within. On the left page was a drawing of the event, and the right page contained the corresponding text. She typed something on the page where the drawing was, and at that instant the ceiling of the dome became a realistic scene of a blue sky with white clouds, moving very slowly. At the same time, on the circular wall of the dome, another realistic scene was projected--a desert with a weak, whistling wind, slightly displacing rocks on the cracked ground. Above the ground, a realistic image of Niskala (from her waist up), in a red dress, materialized. Her back was facing the audience, her face the distant horizon. The wind blew her hair and dress slightly. Then, the wind became more quiet and stopped blowing. Rocks, hair, and dress, stopped moving too. Adiana said:

"An immeasurable desert was ahead of Niskala. Underneath her feet, cracked, barren land. Above her, white clouds and blue sky. In the distance ahead, she saw a stairway leading to heaven, its top disappearing in the clouds." Everything that Adiana was describing in words was appearing in the same order in the scene. "Some stairs were white, some black. Suddenly, from the black stairs screeching crows and ominous bats flew out. Black growling panthers jumped out with poisonous frogs. Black, hissing, rattle snakes crawled out. The army of darkness, never touched by light, was coming closer and closer to attack Niskala. She took her sphere of skalium..."

And that's where Adiana paused for a moment, shocked with what she read next in the book. Without vocalizing it for the audience, she read, to herself, the next paragraph that was completely inaccurate. It depicted something that did not happen, something contrary to Niskala's personality and views. What Adiana knew for fact was that Niskala's sphere divided into many smaller ones, creating a wind, whose force pushed the animals away from her; however, in the book, something else was written: it said that the sphere divided into many smaller inflamed ones that flew towards animals and cut them in half, and that animals lay dead in puddles of blood. That description was too dramatic and detailed; it was highly unlikely that it was an innocent mistake.

In that paragraph, Adiana saw a lie, a deliberate distortion of the truth. She wondered why Niskala would write something like that. She finished the story in the way she knew it, following the truth. Nobody noticed, for a moment, that Adiana's attention wandered, and she successfully managed to suppress her confusion and shock. After the sermon, she immediately went straight to Heliopolis.

"Niskala," Adiana addressed Heliopolis, somewhat angrily.

"Yes, dear?" Niskala's voice responded.

"What is going on with the book? What's written in there is not true. You did not kill the animals. Why is it written that you did?" She demanded an answer.

The voice paused. Then it said: "I know, dear Adiana. You are right. During my earthly life, I did what you said I did; I was a peace-maker and did not kill anyone. However, now I see further and better, with my new cosmic eyes. Now I know that I did not do the right things while I was mortal. I had a veil across my eyes, the veil of idealism. Now that the veil is off, I know I would kill all those animals since they deserve it," Niskala's voice explained.

Adiana could not believe what she was hearing. She absolutely disagreed with Niskala's voice, and still shocked, she asked:

"Shall people be taught that they need to be aggressive? That there is no defense that just deflects someone's attack? That there is no remorse? No forgiveness? That there is no second chance?"

"Yes, Adiana. That's right," the voice calmly said. "People need to learn that their defense needs to consist of bringing death to the opponent. And the one who attacks first, will not only deflect that attack, but the attacker will be killed, annihilated. Not an eye for an eye, and a tooth for a tooth—those are signs of weakness, but death for an eye and death for the tooth." Adiana was speechless and the voice continued:

"When someone has fear of annihilation, only then will that person not even think about harassing, bullying, and attacking another person, initiating wars, and becoming a criminal. Fear is the best prevention, my child." Adiana did not know what to say; she never expected this from Niskala.

"I know, dear Adiana, that you do not see this now and that you are against it, but just try to understand that I see further than you do. I just want the best for this world and for you—that's all. I'm sure you are aware of it," the voice said.

Adiana was wise. She did not want to get into a deeper discussion and a possible confrontation since she was beginning to understand what was going on here. This could not be Niskala, no way. And even if it were Niskala, then something drastically changed about her since she now believed in principles that were so foreign and repulsive to Adiana as well as the Niskala she once knew and loved. Adiana still loved Niskala, the old one, but this new one—this entity pretending to be Niskala—she couldn't accept any longer.

"Maybe you are right Niskala," Adiana chose her words wisely. "Most likely you do see further than I do. I just need some time to accept some things... this change. Do you mind if I leave Heliopolis and start preparing my next sermon?"

"Not at all, go ahead my child. I am very sorry that I overwhelmed you with my new worldview. I hope you will forgive me. But, everything changes, dear. Me too. Soon, you will be very enthusiastic about your new views too. You'll see," the voice said cordially. Adiana faked a smile and left Heliopolis.

Adiana suspected that this new religion about Niskala was based on real events, but the made-up inserts were true poison. Who knows how many of these poisonous modifications exist in the book. And who wanted to influence people to become violent? Who wanted to regress human beings? Why? She wondered. Also, she became convinced that the voice could not belong to real Niskala. She wondered if someone else was creating the voice, with the technology of the spheres and pulling her into its spider web of lies, attempting to brainwash her. The voice must have been a fabrication, and the cause of this illusion was someone with totally opposite views from Niskala. And did Niskala even die? Perhaps she was imprisoned somewhere. Perhaps Nel, Icarus, and Niskala were alive, trying to liberate themselves. Perhaps they needed help.

Since Adiana now needed time to identify the cause of this conspiracy, she decided to pretend that she accepted "Niskala's" views, until she found a way to defeat this shrewd opponent. She only knew that the opponent was extremely dangerous since it succeeded in removing Niskala, who was the symbol of wisdom and carefulness. Adiana also knew that at some point she would not be able to pretend any longer, that she would renounce this new religion, but what would be the consequences of that? She did not have the slightest idea. She suspected that if this new religion took off, and it was already becoming very popular, the people would be in grave danger. As a result of this new religion, there could easily be blood-spilling and war. That was obvious to her since the new creed had a blatantly aggressive orientation, which people would justify and embrace since it was, supposedly, endorsed by their trustworty and wise Niskala. Adiana also reflected on the idea of one priestess per sanctuary. Who knows how many of them would take for granted what's written in the "Holy" book. Adiana did not have much time, and she knew that very well. So, she had to act. Fast.

CHAPTER THIRTEEN

HOLY RELIC

That entire night, until morning, Adiana spent reading the book, page by page, sentence by sentence. She was horrified at how much distortion of truth and lies were there. Many events were completely made up, accomplishing quite the opposite effect of what Niskala believed and taught others during her life. Often, the paragraphs of the book justified disunity, envy, aggression, blind obedience to authority, prejudice and discrimination, as well as intolerance of other religions, races, and ethnic groups.

For instance, in reality, when Niskala was making birdhouses with children, her intention was for children of different ethnic groups and races to work together, to mix, to do something creative and noble together. She wished for them to enjoy their play, while liking each other's company, exploring each other's similarities and differences, without placing an importance on the concept of race or ethnicity. That entire process was supposed to be their main reward. Niskala was very successful in fulfilling her intention. However, now in the "Holy Book," all of that was turned upside down; the event was described in a very different, untruthful way, as if Niskala divided the children into groups: Children with white skin in one group, those with darker skin in another, and children with slanted eyes in another. It stated that Niskala gave them a task to complete, and that she said that the group with the best birdhouses would receive a reward. Adiana saw in that the seeds of racism, an idea that one race was superior over another.

In another place in the book, children were flying in the sky with Nel and Icarus, who taught them how to use wings. The book explained that Nel and Icarus forbade children from holding hands, teaching them that they needed to be independent and to always count on themselves alone. The children were never allowed to hold each other's hands or the hands of Icarus or Nel. The book advocated for disunity and extreme independence. In reality, however, Adiana knew very well that the situation was the opposite—rarely had Nel and Icarus told the children not to hold hands to get a sense of independence; on the contrary, holding hands was encouraged and emphasized to foster the idea of support of others, interconnectedness, and unity.

One chapter in the book was about the invention of the element skalium. According to the book, Niskala was a member of a team of researchers who worked on this project. At the moment when the element was to be named, Niskala, without any consultation with others, proclaimed: "We'll call it *skalium*, after me, your great Niskala." In the book, all present accepted that name joyfully, without any debate or consideration of any alternatives. However, in reality, it did not happen like that at all. The researchers believed that the element should be named *Niskalium* after Niskala, to honor her; also, the name was easy to remember, and it sounded good. They recommended the name to Niskala, so she could decide. She, however, thought that it was not fair to name their accomplishment after her since many other people contributed to the project. She advocated for finding a different name that was not associated with her name only. She proposed a vote, and the majority voted for a compromise—*Skalium*. It was clear to Adiana that the book was sending a message to people to blindly follow their leaders' opinions, without disagreeing with them or offering alternatives.

Another part of the book reflected the same message. In reality, when the first Heliopolis was about to be built, Niskala asked the citizens where they would prefer the city be erected. The majority of the people voted that the location be in front of Niskala's castle since everyone liked being near her. Niskala never imposed her wishes. She believed in communication, compromise, presenting arguments, and their analyses. She encouraged different perspectives and always supported a voting process. In the book, however, she was the only one who single-handedly decided about the location. There were many other examples of the book's toxicity. After she was done reading the book, Adiana washed her hands thoroughly and for longer than usual, as if she were cleansing herself from all the evil she encountered in it.

Adiana felt tense, due to the book's dangerous content and the entire situation, and she could not fall asleep. She kept thinking about what to do, trying to figure out a solution to all of this newfound information. Close to dawn, she managed to fall asleep, briefly. She had the same dream that was haunting her ever since Niskala's death, except that this time, for the first time, she heard what Niskala was saying in that dream much clearer. Adiana saw the rough sea carrying Niskala on her wings. She held a miniature sphere close to her mouth, talking to it: "Do not read holy books about me. If you have already read them, burn them... Do not paint holy pictures with my image in them, and do not draw a halo above my head.... Do not build sanctuaries with my name on them..." Niskala continued to talk, but it was not comprehensible any longer, due to the sound of waves, thunder, and the shrieks of birds. Adiana saw the fingers of Niskala's wounded, bleeding hand, holding the tiny sphere, bringing it closer to a feather of the wings underneath her. The sphere transformed into a tiny feather and inserted itself among the remaining feathers, as if Niskala wanted to hide it there, to camouflage it. It was as if the sphere was very important, and contained some essential information.

Adiana abruptly woke up... she had an idea... Perhaps this dream wasn't just her imagination after all. Perhaps what she heard in her dream was really spoken by Niskala, and maybe that same sphere existed too. Adiana thought how important it would be to get hold of Niskala's final words, especially to obtain her entire speech. Adiana suspected what the nature of the entire speech was and how crucial it would be.

She couldn't wait for dawn to break so she could hurry to Heliopolis. But, she didn't want to go there too early, to avoid looking suspicious. She could not reveal that something was bothering her. Whoever was behind the voice could not suspect that she had a plan and that she was burning to implement it. As usual, before the opening of Heliopolis in the morning, she walked in and went to the area where she usually stood when she communicated with the voice. And she said:

"Dear Niskala, I know how to improve your religion and attract even more followers."

"Really? I am delighted that you thought about that, my dear. So, how would you attract more followers?" the voice asked.

"Each one of your sanctuaries should have a Holy Relic, something that remained after your death, that survived you, something associated with you during your last moments, when you died for the benefit of others. That something would have the same power as the Holy Book and the sanctuary, if not even more power to attract people with its sacredness. The people would flock to the sanctuary to see the Holy Relic, to touch and kiss it. Through their contact with it, they would become closer to you."

"And what would that be, dear? That Holy Relic?" the voice asked.

"Your wings! They were made to be virtually indestructible. They may be damaged, but not destroyed or completely lost. I'll go and look for them in the same area where you lost your life. I'll find them and return with them—I'll bring you the Holy Relic." Adiana spoke with such passion and enthusiasm. She knew that it was best to ask for permission. Leaving without asking would likely mean being stopped since it was obvious that the voice was an expression of someone or something sinister with the need to control everything.

But Niskala's voice was silent... Seconds seemed to last for hours for Adiana. She feared that she had overdone her performance and that the voice saw right through her. Then the voice said:

"Great idea! Yes, bring me the Holy Relic. It would be best for you to leave tomororw morning since I would like to ask you to deliver your sermon today, here in Heliopolis. Did you see when you came in? I built them last night? Aren't they breathtaking?" the voice asked.

"No, I haven't seen anything. I was so excited to tell you about the relic that I didn't notice anything else." Adiana turned around... she saw sanctuaries, each one identical to the one she built in the field of red poppy flowers. Now ten of them were in the parks of Heliopolis. Real Niskala would never do that, such an expansion of her religion, since she would keep everything in balance. In Heliopolis, years ago, the real Niskala already erected a dome dedicated to religious tolerance, where visitors could experience presentations of *all* world religions, under the same dome, during the equal timeframes. The real Niskala would add, in addition to other religions, her own religion, making it equally important; however, this abomination, this exaggerated presence of one religion over all others, was a clear message that the new religion was the most important and most needed one—above all others. That self-centeredness and expansion looked to Adiana to be a gruesome act of conquest by someone with no respect for other faiths. Adiana despised all that but had to pretend that she was embracing it.

"How magnificent!" she said. "I can't wait to step into each one of these amazing sanctuaries. Oh, how wonderful they are; they really improve Heliopolis. Niskala, do you have anything against my leaving now to look for the relic? I am inspired now and highly motivated. Almost all religions have some Holy Relic, why would yours be without it? My search should not be delayed even for a second more. I think we should continue with sermons when I am back with wings, when the impact on people is more powerful. I know I will find them. I will turn every rock to recover them and bring them to you." Adiana was hoping for a positive answer, to leave immediately since she could not deliver even one more sermon in the sanctuaries built on lies. She could not read any more from the book of evil. But, the voice was silent.

"I had a clear vision, Niskala. The most beautiful one," said Adiana, trying to spark the voice's curiosity to eventually grant her permission to leave. "A miraculous one."

"What kind of vision?" asked the voice. Adiana's plan seemed to be working.

"I am standing on the top of a mountain, looking at Heliopolis in the distance. And I'm thinking... The human race has overcome Heliopolis. Heliopolis, as is, is obsolete. Haven't human beings already made progress with its help? What else, what more can we learn from it? And I said to myself: We are ready for the next big step, the next level. Niskala's religion. That's the next step, a level higher than Heliopolis, a step higher than any other religion that ever existed since the beginning of time. Your religion would open the door to a new existence where the horizon broadens to the most magnificent realizations." Adiana was pretending convincingly. She was telling the voice what it wanted to hear, things she knew that the voice already planned to do. The voice was silent, so Adiana continued:

"I see domes and pyramids of Heliopolis disappearing... dividing into whirlpools of spheres that fuse with the walls of this city. The activities that are happening in them evaporate. Heliopolis, as such, disappears too. But, where the old one stood, a new one, an even more magnificent one arises, from the old's ashes. That entire new Heliopolis becomes *your* sanctuary. New Heliopolis of Holy Niskala. No other religion exists there, only yours." Adiana said and continued:

"And I see people, who, like rivers, come from all sides into Heliopolis, to be as close as possible to you, to their Niskala, to merge with you, to live in you as you live in them. I see myself standing above all of them, holding the Holy Feather from your wings, and I lower it on their heads... and as the Holy Feather touches them, I see a transformation in their eyes—eternal happiness and peace. Their feelings of unity with you, their Holy Niskala. You are their salvation from pain and worries; you are their bliss. This vision," she added, "is the sign that we cannot postpone my search for the Holy Relic any longer. We need it as soon as possible." The voice didn't say anything for a few seconds, then it spoke:

"You don't speak any longer as a priestess, Adiana." The voice paused. Adiana was stunned. Did she go too far in her pretense? Was she uncovered?

"You speak like someone who overcame that level... You are a prophet, my dearest child." The voice continued. "Your vision is a glimpse of the future. Go, go, and find me the wings, and come back here to your home, to me, to your second mother."

"Thank you, Niskala." Adiana bowed for the first time, pretending that she was a subordinate. She knew that this new gesture of bowing would be liked by the one who created the voice, that the person would think Adiana accepted her servitude and that she wanted to prove herself to the master.

CHAPTER FOURTEEN

THE CAVE

Adiana flew over the Lacrimal Sea, along the coordinates where Niskala, Icarus, and Nel were last seen. Not too far ahead, the rough part transitioned into a calm one. It seemed logical to her that the wings ended up on that side, since the waves from the rough part moved towards the calm one. Behind the line, where the serene side started, she saw islands. Perhaps the wings reached one of them, she thought. The inhabitants probably knew about their whereabouts. She was heading towards the closest island.

When she reached the calm side, down below her, were several boats with fishermen throwing their nets into the sea. She hoped they knew something about Niskala's wings, so she started her descent towards them. The fishermen noticed her when she was close enough, and when they recognized who that was—their Adiana—with large smiles they waved towards her. She landed on the first boat.

"Adiana? What an honor, this is... what a big surprise," the fisherman said, forgetting the net he was pulling out. "This is better than catching the fish that fulfill wishes," he joked, wiping his hands on his clothes and approaching Adiana, not knowing whether to hug her or shake her hand. She made a step towards the fisherman and hugged him, smiling. She touched a sphere on the front of her jacket, and the wings retracted into a disc on the jacket's back.

"Good morning," she said. "I am looking for Niskala's wings. Do you, perhaps, know anything about them?"

"Yes, sure. The fishermen found them after... after what happened to her. They found three pairs of wings, actually... Nel's and Icarus's too," he said with a sad expression. "I still cannot believe what happened," he said, shaking his head.

"Me neither," Adiana said with a despondent face, placing her hand on his shoulder. "Do you, perhaps, know what they did with the wings?" she asked.

"They took them to a cave... Next to that island over there," he pointed to one. "It is a small cave, on a long strip of sand. Children used to play in it, but now the wings are there. Every day, lots of people go there to see them. We have felt a bit better ever since we have had something from Niskala, Nel, and Icarus, something we can touch," the fisherman said. "I can give you a ride to the cave if you like. I would be honored," he said.

"That would be so nice of you. Thank you," said Adiana. The fisherman started the engine.

He took her around a nearby island, where a long strip of sand extended from the island to a rock with an opening in it. Many people walked on the strip, forming a line, slowly moving forward then stopping for a few minutes, waiting for those who entered the rock to pay their tributes and leave.

"Do you mind letting me borrow your hat?" Adiana asked the fisherman. "I would like not to attract any attention today since I don't have that much time."

"Certainly. Here you go. You can keep it, it's my present to you," and the fisherman handed her his large hat. She tied her hair up and put the hat on. Now, it would be very difficult for someone to recognize her.

"Thank you for everything." Adiana hugged him and stood in the line with the others. Even though she was the world's leader, and pressed for time, she wanted to wait, to show respect to other people in line. When her turn came, she entered the rock.

Inside, it looked like a cave, with just enough light rays coming in through the cracks in the stone. Attached to the wall, there were three pairs of spread wings. She recognized all three--one belonged to Icarus, the other one was Nel's and the third one Niskala's. Adiana placed her hand on Icarus's wings running her fingers through its feathers. She turned to Nel's, doing the same. Then she approached Niskala's... Adiana looked at them, leaned her cheek against them, spilling a tear over the feathers.

"Oh, my dear Niskala," she said, running her fingers through the wings. She wiped her tears, made a few steps back and stood facing the wings. Then she spoke in the language of the spheres:

"Taela saluma e sa di Niskala etuma hisi o liuma?" In translation it meant, "What sphere was the last one Niskala inserted among the feathers?"

As she pronounced those words, each feather lit up, but only one detached from the wings, slowly falling towards the floor. While still in the air, it became a miniature sphere that flew straight to Adiana's palm. She said:

"All spheres in the room, except the one on my palm, turn off." She wanted to prevent any possibility of being spied on through skalium technology. Then she addressed the sphere in her hand. "Show me what Niskala said before she put you among the other feathers. Disable any transmission outside this place." Suddenly, the sphere emitted a beam of light, narrow like a laser, then it expanded into a screen, displaying the recording of the last few minutes of Niskala's life. Adiana paid attention to every word, every detail, without blinking. She listened with sadness, but also hope and excitement. She knew that this message would change everything.

She pulled out her necklace, the one that Niskala gave her and said to the sphere: "Join the rest of the spheres on my necklace." And the sphere found its place among them, changing its color and size to be alike the rest. Adiana took off her hat, letting her hair down, and she stepped outside the cave, where the people were waiting in line. They were pleasantly surprised when they recognized her. She said:

"My dear friends, I came only to get Niskala's wings, with your permission, of course. I know how much they mean to you, and I promise to return them soon. I need them to accomplish something very important. Can you please allow me to take Niskala's wings? I will understand if you say no."

"Of course, Adiana," someone said.

"Sure, Adiana, take them," another person added, and the rest of them agreed.

"Thank you very much, my friends." She put the hat on a child's head, making him very happy, and she returned to the cave, where she detached Niskala's wings from the wall and brought them outside. As she walked through the line of people, all those who were waiting to see the wings could now touch them. When she came to the beginning of the strip, she said:

"I'll return soon with the wings." She touched a symbol on the front of her jacket and her wings unfolded from the disc on her back, and she flew away.

CHAPTER FIFTEEN

THE FINAL SERMON

"Niskala, now when we have recovered your wings..." Adiana began, standing in Heliopolis, "...and when each Heliopolis on the planet has ten of your magnificent sanctuaries, the time has come for me to establish the order of priestesses that you spoke so wisely about before. As you envisioned, every priestess will closely resemble me. It is their destiny."

"Yes, Adiana. I agree. The time has come," said the voice.

"Each sanctuary will have a feather from your wings. Every feather will be one Holy Relic. The power of your religion will thunder throughout the world when each Adiana delivers sermons with your Holy Book in one hand and the Holy Feather in the other. The sick will become healthy, the disturbed will find peace again, and suffering will perish, giving way to joy," Adiana explained.

"Your prophecies are so moving, so inspiring, dearest Adiana. That's exactly what the world needs—a prophet like you," the voice said. "And a mighty religion that everyone will faithfully embrace, a religion with countless sanctuaries that will never cease to multiply. Those who did not believe before, will now become believers, and those who used to be believers, will reject their previous creed with contempt towards it, asking themselves how they could have believed in such a charade. The day is coming when all people will rise in the morning and see that this new religion, my religion, is the only sacred truth. Let me ask you something, Adiana."

"Ask, Holy Niskala," Adiana said.

"Which religion has a Holy Book that levitates and shines on people with its tangible light and accepting warmth? Which religion has an indestructible feather for its Holy Relic? Which religion has sanctuaries where the sermon unfolds in front of people's eyes, like real events? Which religion has a sanctuary with a breath-taking dome, in which they see the reflection of their souls, freed from suffering? Which religion has a martyr who was admired by everyone and who improved everyone's lives? Which religion has the martyr whose wounds from sacrificing are so recent and whose death is so unbearable, as it happened only months ago? Which religion has you for the prophet? Which religion will have numerous gems like you? Which religion is so glorious? Tell me, Adiana, tell me?" The voice demanded.

"Your religion, Holy Niskala," responded Adiana, "only your religion."

...

Soon Heliopolis became what Adiana "prophesized." Not a single other religion was represented in the city, only the one of Holy Niskala. In the past, the roads of Helipolis contained large spheres with sculptures of Marie Curie, Nikola Tesla, Albert Einstein, Mozart and many other influential people, yet now, the same glass spheres were furnished exclusively by sculptures of Niskala with a halo.

The order of Adiana-like priestesses, hand-picked by her, was well-trained and ready. In the Heliopolis, the one that was erected first, Adiana conducted the final training. It was a dress-rehearsal for the event that was about to happen in a couple of days. Something very remarkable and extraordinary was about to occur— the Great Sermon, led by Adiana, was to be delivered at the same time by all priestesses in all sanctuaries of all Heliopolises on the planet—the largest religious gathering ever orchestrated in the history of civilization. The priestesses' roles were to mimic Adiana's every word and move—to be her exact replicas.

At the conclusion of the final training before the event, numerous priestesses, dressed-alike, with identical hair color and haircuts, of the same weight and height, were awaiting Adiana's final words, before they were dispatched to their sanctuaries. Adiana addressed them:

"For the betterment of humanity! For Holy Niskala!"

At once, all priestesses, in solemn silence kneeled on one knee, with their heads bowed in the direction of Adiana—it was as if the general were conducting final preparations before the army goes to war. All priestesses, at the same time, stood up, forming a line, approaching Adiana, one by one. On each priestess's shoulder, she placed her hand, looking them straight in eyes, and quietly spoke with a smile:

"For the betterment of humanity."

"For the betterment of humanity!" Every priestess responded, smiling back, continuing to walk, leaving Heliopolis in a line. In just a few days nine of them would return for the Great Sermon, but the rest of them, thousands, would reach the remaining sanctuaries of Holy Niskala, throughout the world.

...

On the day of the Great Sermon, in the sanctuary where Adiana preached, people were sitting, waiting for her to walk in at any minute. Believers throughout the world, in the sanctuaries and in front of television sets, were expecting the sermon to start in exactly three minutes. Punctually, Adiana entered. In all remaining sanctuaries, priestesses did the same, mimicking her every move. The Holy Book materialized in the middle of the domed room. Adiana approached the book and typed something on its covers. In an illuminated mist of miniature spheres, close to the ceiling, a feather began to materialize. It landed on Adiana's palm. Walking with the feather, she touched each person on the head with it. All priestesses did the same. In their vicinity there was a sphere, displaying what Adiana was doing, so they could mimic her behavior. Then, Adiana spoke:

"My dear ones, sometimes it seems that life ends without being finished. Somebody leaves us too soon, suddenly, unexpectedly, and we believe that the life was abruptly interrupted, without completion. This makes us believe in the absurdity of life. But, is that so? Are our lives ever incomplete and abruptly cut short? Perhaps, as much as life seems to be short, it still carries in it an important message for us, perhaps even a crucial, eye-opening one, transforming that short existence into an everlasting one. Sometimes, the most significant messages that can improve our lives can fit in the last minutes or even seconds of life.

Tonight, I will tell you what happened during the last few minutes before Niskala gave her life to save others." Adiana paused, and smiling, glanced over all present in the audience.

"Hit by the relentless pieces of the shattered metal, Niskala fell into the rough sea. Waves were throwing her, threatening to drown her, but she tenaciously held to her wings that supported her on the surface. Her wounds, filled with sea salt, brought her excruciating, agonizing pain, yet she gathered her final ounce of strength to send us her final message, the last words before she closed her eyes."

Adiana pulled out her necklace and detached a miniature sphere, the one that she found in Niskala's wings. Priestesses did the same.

"Show the last five minutes of Niskala's life on the wings in the sea." Adiana commanded the sphere, and on the wall of every sanctuary of the world, Niskala's drama in the sea started to unfold.

Everyone could clearly see Niskala, and hear her last words which were the following:

"Even if I were divine, do not see me as such, and do not worship me. Do not read holy books about me. If you have already read them, burn them and quickly forget the passages you learned. Do not paint holy pictures with my image on them, and do not draw a halo above my head. Do not build sanctuaries with my name on them, and do not flock to them. Do not listen to those who preach about me; instead, turn your backs on them and leave. Do not embrace a religion about me, and sever your ties with it right away. Break your bondages and leave them behind.

If you do not listen to my advice, and if things that I caution you against still come into being, all that will become your weakest spot, a point of your crumbling fall, of a very difficult return, or no return at all. If what shouldn't be comes to be, your eyes will close and your blind obedience will rise. Beings of darkness will easily lie to you preaching that I was what I never was. You will believe both in what I really said and did, and in words and deeds they falsely ascribe to me. You will believe in their stories about my deeds and misdeeds: those that I never did nor imagined ever doing. All sanctuaries, holy books, paintings, relics—the entire religion about me—is their fabrication, like a magician's tricks. Except that magicians use tricks to entertain, while the beings of darkness use them to divide and conquer. During this time when morality, love, and peace rule, they are hungry for human hatred; they crave crumbs of greed, crime, fear, rage, war, and suffering.

To survive, they will hit you in your weakest spot, in your Achilles's heel—and that's me. They will use all that you perceive as sacred about me and turn it upside down, twist it, alter it, desecrate it, yet you will not be aware of any of their wrongdoings. They will persuade you that their blasphemy is something sacred since they are the most skilled liars and the shrewdest among the evil ones, beings of manipulation and pretense, lords of shadows who emerge from darkness, and return to their home that is the night.

When you are thirsty, they will carry you across the river of drinkable water, telling you "don't drink, it is poisonous." Yet, they will give you real poison to drink, calling it the elixir of life, youth, and happiness. You will trust them that black is white and that white is black since they will put a veil across your eyes and alter your vision. Those who murdered me will lie to you and tell you that they are my closest followers and friends.

Your shield, armor, and sword of defense is me: the one that you *should* see. See me as one of you, who walks with you, side by side, being a unique person, just like every one of you. I am a flower of relaxing hope in a field that brings back faith and calmness; a tree of endless life in the forest of eternal living; a grain of intelligence, knowledge, and experience on a sandy beach of wisdom; a regenerating wave of joy in a sea of renewing smiles; a cloud of freedom in a limitless sky; a ray of creation from a source of light that gives birth, nurtures, improves, and heals.

In the most beautiful parts of you lie my strength and my point of origin. To nurture that side of you is my wish and destiny. Unified with your light, I am not afraid of anything, and my death... it is my new beginning." At that point the recording stopped.

In all sanctuaries, without exception, silence prevailed. People in the audience sat in their chairs, as if frozen in time, staring motionlessly at the empty wall in front of them, as if they still saw Niskala speaking her final words, as if her ideas echoed without stopping. Many wept and wiped their tears. But those tears were not only because of the end of her life and her physical pain, no, that sadness was mixed with something else---with a liberating revelation, coming from her last words about how to continue living.

And then, one by one, people stood up, approached Adiana, and hugged her tightly and warmly. They did not say anything.

Adiana said nothing either. Yet, they understood each other perfectly well. Their hugs spoke, instead of their words, reflecting gratitude for this evening, for what Adiana revealed to them. All visitors, in all Heliopolises, in every single sanctuary of Holy Niskala, left with no intention of coming back, ever.

"Let all sanctuaries crumble into spheres, and spheres return to the walls of Heliopolis. Heliopolis, return back to the condition that Niskala left you in before she passed away. Old pyramids and domes, rise!" Adiana commanded.

Very rapidly the sanctuary in which Adiana stood started its self-demolition and reorganization. Spheres were leaving the walls, floor, armchairs and drawings, connecting to build lost pyramids and domes from scratch. They were quickly coming back to existence in the same locations where Niskala had originally put them. Sculptures with the image of Niskala, were gone—they transformed into the sculptures of great men and women who originally contributed to this city's glory.

The sanctuary from which Adiana was observing the rise of the old Heliopolis was almost completely disassembled. On the floor, or what was left of it, from nowhere, the hooded woman in black materialized. She stood motionlessly about 20 steps away from Adiana. Her face could not be seen since the hood covered it. She held a crow, petting it.

"In a few minutes, I can return everything the way it was, but you'll do that instead," the woman said to Adiana. "Or, your parents, Io, and Nora, and you will be dead. First, for seven days you will be possessed by demons, who will suppress your personalities and torture your bodies. You will inflict injuries onto yourself and others; you will eat rocks, pull out your hair; you will break your nails against walls. Your voices will be silenced, and demonic voices will echo through you. On the seventh day, you will die in excruciating pain from hunger and thirst since demons will not let you eat or drink."

"Through centuries," the woman continued, "the process has been perfected. There is no cure. The destiny of those you love is in your hands." She said, placing the crow on the floor, and the bird started to contort, clap its wings, screech, bite itself, and hit the ground with its beak, then he took off flying towards Adiana, with the intention to attack. Suddenly, it just fell down to the ground, next to Adiana's feet, motionless, barely breathing.

"I'm not returning anything," Adiana responded fearlessly. "Especially not now when you lost your followers. You can, however, return to where you came from and take your evil with you. Leave the crow with me, and I'll find a cure for it, just as I found a solution to free people from your deception." Adiana responded.

"Child, you disappoint me. Niskala would react much more wisely," said the woman in black, slowly walking towards her.

"Niskala is Niskala, and Adiana is Adiana," she argued. "We're different, yet *together* we defeated you," Adiana responded.

In the language of spheres, the woman addressed the wall, and two spheres detached from it, landing on her palms in a split second. She ran her fingers over their surfaces drawing a shape, and the spheres turned into daggers. The woman just appeared in front of Adiana, holding the crossed daggers underneath her throat, with the intention of cutting off her head.

"Choose your final words wisely, Adiana. You can still save your life and those you love," the woman said.

"What are you waiting for," Adiana spoke her final words. Furious, the woman clenched the daggers and...

CHAPTER SIXTEEN

RETURN FROM THE AFTERLIFE

A few weeks earlier...

Shortly after the explosion that took away Niskala, Icarus and Nel, Niskala's body slid from her wings, and sunk into the depth of the Lacrimal Sea. It reached its deepest, darkest realm, and gently touched the floor, lying on it, as if it were a comfortable bed made of sand. A source of light appeared in all that darkness, making it look more like a tunnel with an illuminated end. The light was intense, brilliant, yet it was pleasant for her to look into. Her eyes were not hurting. And how would they, when she did not have them any longer. She did not have her body either. Only her soul remained, a subtle entity, composed of personality and consciousness, that left her body slowly moving, spirally towards the light. That wasn't an ordinary light; it was gentle and warm, but not in a physical sense. It loved.

The loving light contained calmness, understanding, protectiveness, compassion, and goodness. It was as if a loving parent was that light. Niskala's soul felt how special and complex the rays were, and she could no longer tell the difference between her soul and the light—they existed as one. On the sand, she saw her body, alone, covered in wounds. But, she did not feel a connection with it any longer; she felt no sadness for it, no regret; in fact, joy and serenity filled her soul, as well as a feeling of unlimited freedom, an absolute absence of confinement. She felt weightless and that she was slowly moving to the light-source. Then, she entered it...

On the other side of the source of light, was a sparkling fog, thick and opaque, that transitioned into a breath-taking landscape. As she exited the fog, she had her body again, completely healed and strong, and she was dressed in a long gown. She was flying over a long, green field with radiant flowers, towards hills and mountains with waterfalls in the distance. Above them was a crystal blue sky with a few white clouds here and there. The temperature was neither hot nor cold; it was very pleasant, perfect. She felt full of energy, without the slightest indication of pain.

Better than ever before she could smell, see and hear things. Her senses sharpened considerably. Remembering Nel, Io, Nora, Icarus and Adiana, she smiled, without being sad that they were not with her any longer, quite the opposite; she was happy knowing that she would see them eventually in this same landscape when the time came for that in the future. Suddenly, her entire life began to unfold in the smallest of details right in front of her eyes. So many years of her life, from her birth until death, were compressed in only a few seconds.

An enigmatic force was pulling her towards a large body of water, located in front of a distant mountain. Soon, she reached that water and realized it was a smooth, barely moving river. In it she saw people, but not that they were bathing, rather some of them were sitting on its surface, and others walked on it. Her flight ended there—the force gently placed her on the surface of the river. As her foot touched the surface, her body began to glow. She stepped into the river, thinking it was shallow, but her foot did not sink, and although she saw fish underneath, she still stayed on the surface as if she were a feather. She walked to the people in the river whose bodies were glowing too. They were calling her, waving at her.

"Welcome, Niskala," someone placed a glowing hand on her shoulder. "I am Jesus. And this is Muhammad. Over there is Buddha. Moses and Isis are approaching us from there. And there is Shiva. And over there... Well, you will meet us all later. There are so many of us that you would spend the entire day meeting us all." Niskala and Jesus laughed.

She put her palm over his hand, and laid her head on his chest. He hugged her, kissed her cheek and gently patted her hair. Smiling, Muhammed and Isis came and hugged her, also kissing her cheek. Buddha approached too and kissed her cheek. Niskala hugged them all back and kissed them on their cheeks.

"I died, didn't I?" she asked.

"No, dear," Buddha explained, "there is no death."

"Only transformation," Muhammad added, "from one energy form into another. Now, you have this form of energy."

"Life is eternal—this body of ours, it is only one of the ways that eternity manifests itself," Jesus said, smiling.

"Where are we?" Niskala asked.

"Another state of existence," Muhammad said.

"And now with you, a much more powerful one," Buddha added.

"With me? I don't understand," Niskala inquired.

"Only you were missing. We waited for you," Moses said, who hugged Niskala and gently touched her hair. "For a prayer."

"A prayer?" she asked.

"A prayer for the change of the demonic heart..." Jesus responded. "They are taking over your planet, creating a religion about you. They are planting lies within that religion that will secure them disunity, slaughter, crimes, fear, wars... everything they need for survival. They feed on that."

"Human darkness is what they are after," Muhammad explained.

"They wrote a book about you," Jesus added, "a book of lies, presenting it as truth, manipulating people."

"How do we defend the world from the demonic invasion?" Niskala asked. "I was no match for such evil."

"None of us is strong enough on our own," Jesus said. "We can defeat them only if we pray *together* to the Divine Source, asking it to transform the demonic soul."

"We can awaken the power of The Source, only if we pray united," Buddha said.

"Our prayer will reach the Source only if we generate enough spiritual energy. With you now, Niskala, we will be able to," Shiva said.

"You were the missing link. We are so happy you are here," Isis added, smiling.

"I understand. Our unity, in prayer, will create the needed energy to activate The Source," Niskala said.

"Yes, dear," Isis said.

Jesus took Niskala's hand and placed her in between himself and Muhammad. With one hand Muhammad held Niskala's, and with the other Buddha's hand. Jesus held Niskala with one hand, and with the other hand Shiva. All sacred beings, held hands, forming a circle so that the circle began in every one of them and ended there too, representing the idea that all of them were equally important for the prayer. Niskala did not need to ask anybody anything about the prayer since she knew it. She didn't know how she knew it, but the words just poured out of her, as if she spoke them many times before. In unison, all of them recited the same words:

"The Divine Source, you who always were and always will be, who exist as Light throughout the universe, taking forms of wisdom, beauty, creativity, and compassion..." As they said these words, their bodies began lowering into the water that covered their ankles.

"...You who inspire and teach us, from whom we came and to whom we will return, please accept our love for the entire universe, for its good parts and for those that are bad." They were up to their knees in water.

"Hear the united voice of many of us who stand in front of You, joined in peace, equality, and love. Accept our radiance that carries within it our loyalty to the truth. Let the rays of our creativity and wisdom find You." The river reached their waists.

"Accept the light of our forgiveness and let our joy about life and gratitude illuminate Your being. Bring to Yourself the glow of our compassion and help to those who suffer." The river reached the line of their hearts.

"Please answer our prayer that everyone who is good becomes even better, and all who were once bad become good, to understand that they used to be evil and why they were evil, to repent, redeem themselves and ask for forgiveness." The river now covered their shoulders.

"Make them respect and love others, feel compassion for others, and induce in them a need to help and protect. And all who became good, make them remain good, and become better, thriving in the light of eternal life." The river reached their chins. Suddenly the river became pure light.

"Please grant our wish and make its embodiment everlasting."

There was no river any longer, neither grass nor flowers, nor mountains or sky. Everything became light that embraced and permeated them completely. Inside that immense field of brilliance, Niskala felt floating weightlessly in the emanation of the Divine Source. Its love, compassion, benevolence and her bliss felt amplified now compared to what she felt standing on the river or spiraling through the tunnel.

The only thing she could discern in that glorious light was the circle of her new friends, holding hands. But they did not feel like mere friends to her any longer; she felt their permanence within her; she felt she was each one of them. She felt that all those different individuals were actually different embodiments of her, the extensions of her own soul. And every one of them had that identical perception of her, she felt. Niskala could easily bring to mind the entire life of every single person in that circle: Moses, Shiva, Isis, the angel Gabriel, anyone, every detail.

Their memories, plans, feelings, everything about them could be revealed to her, only if she wished for that to occur. They too could know everything about her, only if they desired. She did not feel the need to hold anything back about herself; it felt so liberating and empowering to be an open book. They were all welcome to know her, just as she was welcome to know everything there was about them. All beings in the circle, were deeply, intimately connected, fused as one soul, and it was apparent to them that the presence of the Divine Source made that profound and transcending perception happen.

It didn't feel to Niskala that they were still in the river. Where were they? She was curious. Light sensed her need to know and became more transparent, revealing to her glimpses of the cosmos. She saw their circle within this immense light, floating, like an illuminated cluster, somewhere in the star-studded universe. Clouds of gas and dust, and distant planets showed themselves through the light. Then, she saw an infinite number of light rays, like aurora borealis, emanating from this cluster, spreading in all directions, overwhelming the entire universe.

She thought how wonderful it would be for the aurora to become various colors, like a rainbow, and that immediately became so. Her smile became larger, and she giggled like a child, realizing that the Divine Source was letting her participate in its emanation, allowing her to contribute her creativity. The enlightened universe gradually transitioned back to the blue sky and clouds above their heads. The immense light subsided, retracting down their bodies towards their feet, changing back to water. They were standing on the surface of the river again. Gently letting go of each other's hands, they all felt that their prayer was granted. Isis approached Niskala and said:

"Dear Niskala, in the name of all of us present, thank you so much for joining us. If you like, you can return to your people and to all those you love. But, if you like, you can stay with us. It is your decision to make."

"I decide to return; first, to people who need me, and after my mission is complete on earth, I'll be happy to come back to all of you. Perhaps, together we can improve this perfect place." Everyone laughed at her joke, as she waved to all of them with a large smile, and left the river.

She went back in the direction she came from, but this time stepping barefoot on the grass. In the distance there was something, like a large round gate enveloped in a sparking fog revealing darkness. She recognized the tunnel she came through. Close to her, there was a white saddled horse, waiting for her, and looking at her. She approached it, patted his beautiful mane and head, mounted it, and rode it in the direction of the gate. Halfway to the gate, she couldn't believe what she was seeing—Nel and Icarus, sitting on the grass, laughing, talking about something. Their bodies were healed, and they looked healthy and full of energy. There was a wooden cabin near them, probably theirs.

When they saw her approaching them, in her body that was glowing, they were at a loss for words, then their surprise turned to a big smile. Nel stood up and ran to her, so excited to see his Niskala again. She dismounted the horse and ran towards him too, hugging him very firmly and kissing him. She and Icarus hugged too, and she kissed him on the cheek.

"Would you like to go back with me to where we came from?" Niskala asked them. "To the surface of the Lacrimal Sea, to our bodies? Or do you want to stay here in this paradise where you will never lack anything? Whatever you decide, so be it. I must go back, to our people. They need me."

"I'd like to be where you and I will continue to love each other, Niskala," Nel said. "And where Io and Nora will be with us. Whether that's here or somewhere else, it doesn't matter to me." As he said these words, Niskala smiled, happy that he made that decision.

"And I," said Icarus, "I will be where we'll continue to be best friends. So, I'm going with you," he said with a smile, and both Niskala and Nel hugged him. She patted the horse, thanking him for the ride, and the three of them walked towards the gate. As they came closer to it, a strong force pulled them towards it, and it sucked them in, returning them to their bodies on the surface of the serene side of the Lacrimal Sea. They saw an island nearby and swam to it.

"Uncle Jeremy," she said, "your fragrances, they won't help you any longer. They're missing some important ingredients. We brought them for you, please let us in."

"I can't," he said. "There isn't enough room in my house for all of you," he said placing a jacket over his nose; the smell was becoming unbearable.

"I didn't mean in your house," the girl said, "I meant in your heart."

"Who are all of you people?" he demanded loudly, addressing them all. "And what's that glow?" he added.

"We're the light," the girl said, "of those you murdered throughout the centuries." "We're their love and compassion--your missing ingredients. Let us in; we can help you."

"No! I don't need your light," he said, noticeably irritated. "Only your darkness carries a value for me."

Suddenly, all those people in the line and on the ships became a single stream of unified light that, like a fast-moving river, passed through him relentlessly. He fell on his knees from the impact of the overwhelming bliss. What the light carried in itself he felt as a balanced mixture of awe-inspiring love, acceptance, empathy, and forgiveness—something indescribably beautiful, exceeding the ordinary reality, something so calming yet uplifting. In the instant of fusion with light, he felt something rapidly intertwining with the core of his being, some novel elements attaching to his soul, ingredients he never thought could survive there. Then, light materialized back into the countless glowing people and numerous ships on the shore and horizon. For the first time he felt sadness for all of them, sadness, love, and a willingness to help. He gathered strength to rise up, and walked towards the girl, hugging her. And all that smell that was so overpowering seconds earlier, was now easily manageable.

"Why did I take your life, dear child?" he whispered to the girl. "You are innocent. Please tell me; I need to know." He was on his knees matching the height of the girl, stroking her hair.

"You killed my dad. And my sadness for losing him killed me. Murder often does not end where directed, but it claims the innocent too," she said.

"Oh, poor child, that's so true," Jeremy wiped his tears. "I'm so sorry for what I did to you and your family." He raised up, looking at them all, and spoke loudly so that everyone could hear: "I am so sorry for what I did to all of you. I'm so deeply sorry," he said, wiping his tears.

"I *wish* I could bring you back to life, dear girl, and give you back your daddy," Jeremy said. The girl smiled and gently touched his face.

"You just did. For what you cannot do, your *intention* bridges the gap. I have to go now," she said. "My daddy's calling me. Thanks, Uncle Jeremy. " She hugged him firmly and ran towards one of the arriving ships.

"Isabella… Isabella…" A man from the ship was yelling her name and waving at her. He quickly exited his ship, running towards her. And as the father and his child embraced, they slowly faded away, with all the other relieved, smiling souls, and ships that brought them this far. Only Aurora Borealis lingered for a while in the sky, and Jeremy who admired its sublime presence of change.

…

The crossed blades of the daggers were pressing against the skin of Adiana's neck. The woman in black was about to push the blades deeper and cut her throat. Suddenly, thousands of brilliant rays of light, coming from everywhere, overwhelmed them both. That awe-inspiring, blissful light carried within itself love, understanding, compassion, forgiveness, and benevolence. But that light did not come from Heliopolis, it felt to Adiana that it came from somewhere outside. The light was so brilliant and immense that Adiana could only see contours of the woman in front of her, everything else seemed to become that light. Then, the light disappeared and everything that briefly became light returned. The woman froze, dropping the daggers that fell on the floor. Her hands that were about to take Adiana's life a moment ago, now extended into a firm hug. The woman wept; her tears wouldn't stop coming. Sobbing, gasping for breath, she lowered her body towards Adiana's feet, holding her legs, crying over them, burying her face in them. Adiana did not understand what was happening or how to explain that surge of light, but it was obvious that the woman was not pretending. What was the reason for this miraculous transformation, Adiana wondered. An unexpected, sudden change descended upon her soul, perhaps triggered by that light, Adiana thought. What was that light made of? Where did it come from? The light of Heliopolis was inspiring and amazing, but this light felt much more complex, otherworldly.

Adiana felt sorry for the woman's pain, so she gently touched her hood, then helped her stand up. The woman reached for her hood, removing it, and the light of Heliopolis illuminated her face for the first time. Adiana could now clearly see her eyes and the rest of the face, unobscured by the hood. The woman's black clothes gradually turned to white.

"I am sorry, dear child. I am deeply sorry for how evil I was to you. Guilt tears me apart."

"Why were you like that to me? Why did you have to kill Niskala?" Adiana asked. The woman could not respond, she only placed her head on Adiana's chest, crying and remembering. She recalled memories: Her father who beat her up, yelled at her, called her insulting names, made her feel worthless. He did the same to her mother. One night, when she was ten years old, defending herself and mother, she stabbed him with a knife, right in the heart. He collapsed and curled up from the pain. She left him to lie in a puddle of blood, on the verge of death, while he begged for help. Her mother could not help since he had knocked her unconscious. Running away from home, the last thing she saw was her little sister, still a baby in a cradle. Taking a horse from the stable, she rode away, filled with anger and hatred, not only towards her father but for the entire human race. She thought, if her own father was such a brutal monster to her, what could she, then, expect from others?

While the woman was haunted by her disturbing memories, crying on Adiana's shoulder, behind her back something extraordinary happened—Niskala, with her wings, descended from the ceiling. Adiana thought she was imagining it, but she wasn't. It really was Niskala, raised from the dead. Her wings retracted. The woman, crying on Adiana's shoulder, heard steps approaching her, prominent, confident, yet calm steps. Niskala gently placed her hand on the woman's shaking shoulder.

"What you don't know about your father," Niskala said, "is that he survived." The woman calmed down and stopped crying. She could not move for a few moments from the shocking information. Then, she turned toward Niskala, and looking into her eyes, asked in disbelief:

"Survived?" She felt a mixture of relief and anxiety thinking about what he did to her mother and her little sister. Adiana wanted to hug Niskala immediately, but she did not feel it was the right moment to interrupt this conversation. The woman gently placed her hand over Niskala's face and said: "I am so sorry for what I did to you." Niskala placed her hand over the woman's.

"Yes, he survived," Niskala said. "All bloody and in pain, he dragged himself to the crib and managed to lift himself up to see his baby. She looked at him with a smile and curiosity, not knowing anything about him or anyone or anything else. At that moment, the baby spoke her very first words which were "da-da." She touched his hair and face. And in that innocent touch, consisting of the absence of any judgement or disappointment, laid his awakening. More than ever before, he recognized the need a child has to be loved and protected, as he looked at the baby in front of him, your sister. And he deeply regretted not fulfilling those needs and not preserving innocence in his older daughter, in you, who just left him. He cried uncontrollably, fighting his physical and mental pain, but he managed to utter: "I am guilty for losing one daughter, but I won't lose you." He gently caressed the baby on her head. "My darling, my dear angel, I will be different towards you, and you will always receive from me an unconditional love. "From then on, from that moment of awakening, he was exactly that, an exemplary father, always sensitive and responsive to her needs."

Niskala added: "I am so relieved that my sister had a better destiny than I," the woman said, "and that my father saved his soul." Niskala added:

"You initiated your father's change by forcing him to come face to face with death. He accomplished many great things during his lifetime, built things and machines for people, and healed the sick, but he couldn't bear to end his life failing to be a good parent. The baby, too, started his change—she gave him an inspiration to overpower his negative side. You and your sister—together—brought him back to life," Niskala said.

"I am so sad that I didn't get to meet her... my little sister. What kind of life did she have? When did she die? Where and how? I would give my immortality and everything else to be with her again," the woman said.

"That baby... your sister.. " Niskala said, "...that was I. I am your sister."

Adiana and the woman were stunned, speechless. Wiping her tears of sorrow, mixed with happiness, the woman firmly hugged

Niskala, who hugged her back. "My little sister," the woman said, "I'm so sorry for all the bad things I did to you."

"I forgive you," Niskala said without any hesitation, and hugged her sister firmer. "I understand what our father put you through and that it was very difficult to choose another path." Niskala kissed her sister and firmly hugged and kissed Adiana too. Then she spoke to her sister:

"But, it would be important that you apologize to all of humankind, for the millennia of suffering that you caused, and for all lives that you took. It will be easier for them if they hear your apology and sense your remorse. Seeing your change, they will know that all that suffering did not happen in vain and that suffering caused by you ends now. It will be important to address them as soon as possible," and then Niskala showed them the way to the tower.

They went through the lower, dark level of the tower, put their wings on, and all three of them took off, reaching the higher level, the illuminated dome. Its door opened, and they walked to a balcony from which the interior of Heliopolis could be seen. Far below, on the floor, stood many people, shocked by whom they saw—their Niskala, alive and well. Some fainted, some cried out in happiness; others thanked God, and some thought it was a miracle. Niskala typed a code into her sphere, and it positioned itself near her mouth, becoming a microphone. All Heliopolises throughout the world transmitted the live feed of Niskala next to Adiana and the woman.

"My dear ones..." Niskala addressed the people below, seeing in them all of humankind. "If only you knew how much I missed you all." A loud applause thundered through Heliopolis. "I am so glad that I am home again, with all of you. Since I have always shared with you both the good and bad information, this time will be no different. Let me tell you what has happened over the past few months." A loud applause followed.

CHAPTER SEVENTEEN

A CHANGE OF HEART

Night descended upon the rough part of the Lacrimal Sea. On one of its small islands, in a dark, tall tower, Jeremy was sitting in his living room, next to a large fireplace, watching Adiana's sermon on the TV screen. After she delivered Niskala's message, and people left the sanctuaries, the dissolution of the new religion was imminent. He turned off the TV and raised his gaze above the fireplace, to the tall wall with many portraits, reflecting on the situation. A sphere of skalium showed up in front of him, blinking. It was a telephone call.

"Yes?" Jeremy answered very composed.

"You saw the sermon," a female voice said.

"Yes, Delilah. Disappointing. Yet, a lost battle inspires strength to win the war. We shall set plan B in motion."

"Certainly. Soon, Idolatra will execute Adiana. After her death, we will win the election. As we agreed before, you'll become Adiana's successor. I'm calling to ask you if you have any second thoughts about that. In case you changed your mind, Idolatra doesn't mind assuming Adiana's position. You've done it so many times, more than any of us; we thought, perhaps, you needed a break," Delilah said.

"No, no, I like doing it," Jeremy insisted. "Every time it's different. A lot of room for being creative with all that power within grasp." He looked at the tall wall above his fireplace, glancing over the portraits of high priests, presidents, kings, and emperors."

"Which one was your favorite role?" Delilah asked.

"It's difficult to say. When I was Caligula, perhaps. When I entered the Roman Senate on my horse, threatening that the horse would become a better chairman than the present one. I'll never forget the faces of the senators, so insulted, so furious."

"Haha. I remember that. I'm sure you'll surprise us with something new and outrageous this time again. This will be different, though. We live in a new world now: peace, prosperity, cooperation."

"A world of romantic ideals, which are much easier to bring to ruin. Let's bring trouble to paradise, shall we?" But something distracted Jeremy from continuing the conversation.

"Let me call you back," he abruptly discontinued, covering his nose with his hand. "What's this? It was never this strong." He sensed an overwhelming odor of blood, death, and destruction. "Where is it coming from?" He said to himself shaken, reaching for a bottle of cologne, spraying it on his neck.

"Uncle Jeremy... Uncle Jeremy..." He heard the voice of a girl, coming from the outside. Through a large arched window, looking into the darkness of the Lacrimal Sea, he saw numerous glowing ships approaching his island from the horizon. It resembled an invasion.

"Uncle Jeremy... Uncle Jeremy..." The voice persisted. He went to the large, massive entrance door and opened it... In front of him, washed up on the sandy shore, were glowing ships, some looking very old, centuries old, some much newer. He saw countless people in them, disembarking, forming a single line that was approaching his tower. There was a strange glow radiating from their bodies. The first in the line, a few feet away, was a little, glowing girl, the one who was calling him.

"When all of us thought that we are moving along a straight line of progress and success, we were attacked. But, this time by a far superior enemy than ever before—we were attacked by a demonic force. The beauty of Heliopolis, as well as your inspiring development, relaxed me, and I let down my guard. I did not install a moral code into skalium spheres. When they were taken from me by an evil opponent, that same technology that has always helped us, could this time have regressed us for centuries. The demonic force attempted to assassinate me, and planned to create a religion based on my martyrdom. Their goal was to persuade you to believe in Holy Niskala, while they manipulated you through untruthful teachings of that religion. The aim of that manipulation was to disunite you, to stimulate war among you, and to fill you with fear, prejudice, anger, and suffering. You probably ask why? It is because the demons feed on those forms of negative energy. We cannot understand that, but that simply is."

Niskala placed her hand on Adiana's shoulder, looked at her smiling, and continued: "And Adiana, our dear Adiana, she filled the void of my absence with her magnificent presence and action. She accepted the responsibility to save humanity from the demonic invasion. Being wise, she pretended that she supported this new religion in order to gain time and detect a weakness in the enemy, and to find something that would help you abandon the religion. She found my message, which you accepted in such an enlightened way. Adiana saved us. I contributed with my message, but you participated equally when you walked away from the new religion. Together, we deflected the invasion." Loud applause and victorious yells roared through Heliopolis. "I am so proud to be a part of your lives." Niskala's words were followed by euphoric applause. "Adiana would like to say a few words." She moved the sphere closer to Adiana.

"My dear friends, like all of you, I was completely crushed thinking that Niskala was not alive any longer. I needed to believe that she survived, and in that vulnerable condition, the demonic force was able to manipulate me by fabricating Niskala's voice. I was ready to become a firm believer in the religion of Holy Niskala until I realized that this new creed altered facts and changed history, attempting to develop negative tendencies in people that would result in antagonism among you. I realized that the voice could not belong to Niskala, and my plan was for the new religion to lose its followers.

"Thanks to dreams in which I saw that Niskala had an important message for us, I went on a quest for that message. Niskala hid it in her wings, and I uncovered her message. Your reaction to Niskala's final words was magnificent, exactly how Niskala and I hoped you would respond—you abandoned the abomination of this new creed. Like Niskala, it is my highest honor to be one of your leaders since you demonstrated, once again, that human beings are beings of virtue, beings of light. Bravo! Bravo to all of you!" A loud applause echoed through Heliopolis for several minutes.

"When you left the sanctuaries," Adiana continued, "understanding Niskala's message, the demonic force unleashed its evil on me. Two blades were on my neck today, and I almost lost my head. But, at that moment, something happened that defies explanation. The demon changed. Her transformation happened right in front of my eyes. Instead of killing me, the demon spared my life, and begged for my forgiveness. Once a demon, now a humanist like you and me, this woman next to me would like to tell you something. Her name is Idolatra." Adiana moved the sphere to her.

"Dear followers of Niskala's and Adiana's work, I wish I were with you during the process of creating human light, but I wasn't. I was, unfortunately, on the side of darkness. For millennia. I blackmailed states-people, queens, kings, priests, priestesses, and many other people of influence; I gave them money, power, and many other pleasures; I granted them fake keys from paradise, and pretended that I could forgive their sins; I did all that in return for their obedience. I demanded them to keep people in fear, poverty, war, and illness, and they successfully secured all that for me. They provided me with the human fall, with perpetual suffering. I needed it, and I fed on it. Only the energy of your suffering could provide me life.

Sometimes I was a statesperson, a queen, a king, a priest or a priestess to accomplish what I needed. More than forty assassinations were attempted on Adolf Hitler, and he survived every time. How is that possible? It is because I was he. Sometimes I would intuitively feel the coming danger, so I would leave before the assassination took place, and when I did not manage to escape, I used my power to regenerate myself, and all wounds healed in seconds.

Fortunately, darkness in me and my need for it, do not exist any longer. It is not all right to say that my life experiences compelled me to become a being of darkness, that I could not do it differently since I always had the *choice*. The responsibility was always on me, and solely on me. I was ten years old when I made a wrong decision to hold onto anger towards my father. At a crossroads where I could choose the path towards respect and protection of the human good side or towards an all-encompassing hatred of them, I made the wrong choice. I chose hatred since love seemed impossible to me. In my father's actions I saw anger and violence, and those demons blinded me, and I couldn't see that from my mother I received only love and nothing but love. Somebody who does not receive love from either mother or father, obtains it from somewhere else. I deeply regret that I did not see that then, that it is important to choose positive feelings over the negative ones. And I regret that I did not take my father to a doctor when I stabbed him with a knife. I see all that now, but then I couldn't. Back then, I only obeyed my impulse of hatred and anger, instead of focusing on reflection and choosing a different path.

Today, I almost took Adiana's life, and a few months ago, I almost succeeded in killing Niskala, yet both of them forgave me. I am sure that was not easy for them, but they chose that particular path since they knew that anger and hatred would only harm them, and not only them but that negative energy would reflect on all of you via their negative moods. They knew that forgiveness can make one free from destructive emotions.

For the evil acts I committed throughout history, I feel extreme guilt, and I regret them. I am very sorry. I realize my mistakes and I know I will not repeat them. The veil of hatred has been lifted from my eyes. Niskala and Adiana will, from now on, have me as their ally, in case you and they want that. Since I hurt the human race, people should put me on trial. Whatever you want to happen to me, I will embrace it. I still have many powers as I did before, and nobody can keep me here if I don't want to remain here. But now, I have an additional power—the strength of morality. And I will accept your decision.

Now, you will have an opportunity to make your own choice of what happens to me. I am sure your decision will not be an easy one since you are enlightened beings, and your sense of morality will heavily influence what you decide. I hope you will make a better choice, for your own sakes, from the one I made on that crossroad.

Many of you are probably wondering what caused this abrupt change in me. I don't understand it either. I am wondering too. I only know that I became fundamentally different today, as if a miracle happened. Perhaps Niskala will be able to shed light on this enigma for us all. She is the voice of wisdom, so she may know." Idolatra turned towards Niskala, moving the sphere to her.

"Dear sister," Niskala said, "I am very sorry that you and I did not develop side by side, traveling together along the road of goodness, but we cannot change the past and erase mistakes already made. What happened today to you, the transformation of your personality, was nothing less than an intervention of the Divine

Source." Dead silence covered Heliopolis. Everyone wanted to hear what Niskala had to say next.

"When my body died, my soul survived, and I saw Jesus, Muhammad, Moses, Buddha, and many other holy persons. We prayed together to the Divine Source to change demons into beings of virtues. The Source answered our prayer, and with the power of its extraordinary light, this change occurred. The Holy people told me that I could come back to live with you, or stay with them if I wanted. I made my choice, and here I am." Another ovation echoed throughout Helipolis.

"This day," Adiana added, "was full of turns and surprises, so let's continue in that same spirit. We have two more pleasant surprises for you. From the dead, with Niskala, return our beloved heroes Icarus and Nel." People were yelling, whistling and applauding relentlessly. Nel and Icarus came from the dome and joined Niskala, Idolatra and Adiana, who were all smiling towards the joyful crowd. After some time, the five of them left the balcony. What an ubelievable day, everyone was saying. Something to remember forever.

CHAPTER EIGHTEEN

PEOPLE'S VERDICT

Somewhere in the Lacrimal Sea, where its wild side transitioned into the serene one, there was a small, uninhabited island. For the purpose of Idolatra's trial, the island was created by spheres of skalium. The island was at the crossroads of two cobblestone roads, also created by spheres; one road was leading from the island towards the horizon, and the other one, leaving the island in the opposite direction. Both roads ended in the sea. They did not connect the island to the land. Thus, the roads held a purely symbolic function.

The island was tiny, only big enough for a massive, wooden desk with chairs in which sat Niskala, Nel, Icarus, and Adiana. Above each of their heads was a sphere, functioning as a microphone and a camera. The event was broadcast throughout the world. A few feet away from them, on the other side of the table, was another massive wooden chair occupied by Idolatra. Above her head was the same type of a sphere. She was awaiting her judgment that was about to be delivered. Nel moved back his chair, stood up, and addressed humankind, reading from a sheet of paper:

"Today we gathered on this point in between darkness," he pointed to the rough side, "and light," and he pointed to the calm side. "Between chaos and harmony. Between the negative part of the human race, which dominated a good part of our history, and the current, positive part, which may shape our future. This point, where we are now, together as the human race, is the moment of our *choice*. The choice has already been made by the majority of voters, and we will announce it today. Behind us is a road that we crossed to get to this point. Ahead of us, however, is the road of our destiny that we determine today by making that particular choice. We will reveal humanity's judgment over Idolatra today," he pointed to her and continued, "standing at a similar crossroads, she once stood. We will see today if we choose the road of hatred, coldness, mercilessness, and a lack of empathy or the road that leads to understanding, reconciliation, and forgiveness. Will we allow our own demonic side to possess us? Or will we disentangle ourselves from that evil part within ourselves?" Nel sat down. Adiana stood up and read:

"Everyone who is ten years old and older had an opportunity to write a rationale about what judgement Idolatra should receive and why. Computer analyses of millions of such essays provided us with a single text representing a pattern that over 90% of the participants displayed in their writing. The judgment consists of alleviating and aggravating circumstances that both influenced Idolatra's behavior. Also, the judgment consists of specific guidelines regarding what will happen with Idolatra from now on." Adiana sat down. Icarus stood up and read:

"I will first introduce you to the extenuating circumstances." He paused for a moment, then continued: "Being ten years old, Idolatra was not mature enough to choose the path of righteousness. Faced with her father's abuse, she was deprived of his continuous love. This treatment influenced hatred and anger towards humans to nest in her. Today, however, Idolatra is a completely different person, a warm individual who deeply regrets her past wrongdoings.

The aggravating circumstances are the following: she chose the way of hatred towards people. That decision put her on a wrong path and blinded her, instead of developing in the direction of love, respect, and compassion. She deepened her hatred, instead of overcoming it. Her hatred, at that point, metastasized into a basic need to feed on human darkness, to feed by taking human lives intentionally, and willingly inflicting suffering on people.

Although Idolatra is today a radically different person, the aforementioned facts about her evil deeds still remain and cannot be merely overlooked, forgotten or erased. We cannot pretend that Idolatra's past was not real, that it doesn't exist. Further, Idolatra did not voluntarily decide to change recently—she did not wish to become a better person; instead, her transformation was caused by external factors, by those who prayed for her change, a prayer answered by the Divine Source." Icarus sat down. Niskala stood up and said:

"Due to the aforementioned alleviating and aggravating circumstances, people find Idolatra to be *guilty*. Therefore, the judgment will consist of the following: Idolatra will dedicate eight hours per day, from 9 am to 5pm, except weekends, to a humanitarian effort for which she will not be financially compensated. Her humanitarian work will consist of helping the staff of institutions, such as hospitals, fire departments, and organizations dedicated to coping with natural disasters. However, if an emergency arises during the weekend, it will be her duty to help. Idolatra will be obligated to do this type of work for as many years as she was harming humans—which is 7,000 years, from the beginning of written civilization until now.

In terms of her material possessions, Idolatra will have only the clothes that she is wearing now. She will be deprived of any other possessions. She is able, however, to obtain additional material possessions through the charity of those individuals who are not her family. In this way, Idolatra will depend solely on compassion of unknown individuals, which will motivate her to develop appreciation and love for humans' good side.

Further, she will be able to visit Io and Nora, her sister's children whenever the children want to be visited by her, but only after Idolatra is done with her daily obligations towards humanity. After 7,000 years of her redemption, she will be forgiven by humankind.

Idolatra, do you have anything to say in regards of this judgement?" Niskala asked.

"Yes, I do," she responded. "For a person who has morality, as I do now, there is no judgment that hurts more than the judgment of my own awakened conscience. Your judgment, dear good people, is very mild in comparison to the guilt I am feeling. I am learning that one is the fiercest judge of him or herself. I am very thankful for the opportunity to redeem myself and for your possible forgiveness that may ensue. I am also thankful and humbled that you gave me an opportunity to learn about the good side of humanity and to be able to improve it further. Thank you for your kind ruling, which reflects your belief in my potential, in everyone's capacity, to be different from what I used to be," Idolatra said.

"Dear friends," Adiana added, "with our judgment, we demonstrated a high level of ethical thinking—we chose the best option, the one produced by our enlightened minds. Icarus, Niskala, Nel, and I are very proud of being members of the human race. This is a day when, once again, our light triumphs over our darkness."

In a few minutes, the majority of the spheres that made up the island, were high in the sky, following Adiana, Niskala, Idolatra, and Icarus on their way home. Before joining them, Nel wanted to stay a bit longer on the disappearing island. . . thinking . . . gazing into the sea. Cobblestone roads were breaking down into spheres, the tables and chairs too. The island was rapidly fading into the spheres. Hovering with his wings above the almost-gone ground, Nel still looked at the sea, at the rough side and at the calm. Those two halves, he thought, are like the human soul. Those sides are possibilities for destruction and evil, and for something good and constructive. And every one of us, he thought, has the freedom to decide whether our positive side will prevail and express itself or not.

CHAPTER NINETEEN

PERSISTENCE OF LIGHT

After the judgment, Idolatra was spending a lot of free time in Heliopolis. She listened to Niskala's advice to do so, and it was not long before Idolatra experienced the power of the city. It seemed miraculous since not only did it induce a positive mood in her and some new insights about life, but it also took away her painful memories. After a couple of weeks of exploring what Heliopolis had to offer, she could not recall anything bad related to her past. Even the slightest bad memory was gone.

It cannot be said that the city was miraculous literally since, in essence, its power was based on science—negative memories (just like any other memories) are biological processes of the cells in the brain. When such processes become inhibited or blocked with other cellular processes, such as those that represent positive experience in Heliopolis, then oblivion and a good mood result. However, there was a dome in Heliopolis in which a person could reestablish a connection with lost memories.

Idolatra entered that dome. The room was illuminated with dim lights created by skalium spheres, and in the middle of the room, from the ceiling to the ground, stood a beam of light.

"Should you decide to enter the light beam," Idolatra heard a male voice say, "events from your past will be revealed to you. Here, you can rediscover lost memories, clarify the vague ones, see the beautiful ones again. Regardless of whether you encounter good or bad memories, the aim is always the same—focus on the positive in them."

She approached the beam, as the voice spoke:

"Everything that you experienced as negative in your life still exists in you, although you cannot remember it any longer. With its positive influence on you, Heliopolis relocated that negative material to your subconscious mind... for now."

"For now? What happens later?" Idolatra asked.

"Soon, Heliopolis will cause the negative memories to dissolve completely and disappear from you. That content is now just not accessible for you, hidden in secret chambers of your mind, but soon all that will vanish," the voice explained.

"How does Heliopolis do that?" she asked.

"Negative mental processes—some thoughts and feelings, for example, exist in the form of cellular processes in your brain. However, your positive experiences in Heliopolis stimulate cells to block and degrade those processes. Similarly, the same positive experience stimulates cellular processes representing the positive experience, so that only those processes occur in the brain." The voice paused, then continued:

"Before entering the light, two options are ahead of you: the first one is to see your life in its entirety, good and bad events. If you choose that option, you will refresh all bad memories; they will resurface in their full intensity from your subconscious and become easily retrievable. But that is temporary since, provided that you spend more time in Heliopolis, bad memories will re-enter the subconscious and soon after disappear from you. The second option is to only see positive events."

"I choose to see my entire life," Idolatra said. She was curious about her past because she could not completely recall its complexities any longer. Did she do something bad in her life, and to whom, she wondered. She entered the light. Suddenly, 7,010 beams of light descended from the ceiling to the ground, containing in them three-dimensional scenes, without sound, and she realized that those scenes were her life. Each beam was one year of it. She could not believe what she was seeing.

"In order to pause a scene, touch the beam. If you want sound, say 'sound,'" the voice instructed her. "Say 'forward,' and the scene will fast forward, say 'back,' and the scenes will rewind. Say 'faster' or 'slower' to control the speed of the scenes. If you want the scenes to be organized according to certain people, events, or locations, just state that, and the scenes will follow your command," the voice said.

Idolatra was shocked with what she saw. She fell on the floor, crushed, tears pouring down her cheeks. Shame and disgust overwhelmed her.

...

When Idolatra returned home, she called Niskala with a shaking voice and asked to see her as soon as possible. Niskala sensed the urgency and visited her sister in a tiny guest house attached to a windmill. The miller was kind enough to offer his guest house to Idolatra. She was lying sick on a couch, and Niskala sat next to her.

"Sister," Idolatra spoke, "the things I saw in the dome with beams, I cannot describe in words. I am sick to my stomach... I want to forget immediately what I saw. Is it possible that that's who I was? That monster?"

"That was your past, sister. You are a different person now," explained Niskala, taking Idolatra's hand in hers. "Don't worry, the memories will disappear after a few days in Heliopolis."

"Will I remain the person I am now? Or will I turn again into the terrifying creature I used to be?" Idolatra asked.

"This is permanent, don't worry, dear. When I prayed for the change of your heart, we prayed for eternal change. I know it concerns you whether you will remain who you are now, but I think I know how to help you have peace of mind."

"How can you help me? We cannot know the future with certainty. Heliopolis showed me the beams of my future life, and my future looks good, but foretelling one's future is only a prediction of a *likely* course of action; it is a *probable* calculation, not a fact. Heliopolis told me that too," Idolatra said.

"True. But, in a few days you will celebrate your thirtieth day in Heliopolis. Then, your ceremony will start. It will show you, very vividly, that your soul is noble and wonderful now and that there is nothing left from your past in it. You'll always remember the ceremony; it will always be a salient reminder of who you are now. That awe-inspiring sight will be deeply imprinted in your mind, and it will always motivate you to maintain and treasure your soul, now a gem. Even if you are ever tempted to do something bad, the memory of the ceremony will give you strength to resist the temptation, to choose the right path, and to believe that you are capable of that choice," Niskala said.

"What's the ceremony about?" asked Idolatra.

"You will see," Niskala said smiling, and hugged her sister.

…

Within Heliopolis stood a tall tower composed of white spheres. Idolatra was in front of it. The windows were vertical, elongated and tinted. On the top of the tower was a circular balcony with a dome in the middle of it. Idolatra entered the tower and encountered the anticipated darkness. A minimal amount of light was coming in from the windows, just enough to allow a person to discern what was what. Coming from above, a beam of faint light illuminated a pair of wings laying on a pedestal.

"You may put the wings on and follow the stairway of light," a female voice spoke. Idolatra put them on.

There was a tunnel above her, leading up. Within the tunnel were rays of light, appearing and disappearing, creating an impression of a lighted spiral stairway. At the end of this tunnel, high above, was darkness. The wings lifted her up towards it. Where the light stairs stopped, the wings gently placed her on the ground. Her eyes quickly adjusted to darkness. What she was expected to do, she did not know. She was waiting for some instruction. Her wings did not retract... for now.

"This is the final stage of your experience of Heliopolis. Are you ready for the ceremony?" She heard Niskala's voice, coming from behind her. Then she felt Niskala's palm, gently landing on her shoulder.

"Yes, I am," Idolatra responded.

"The ceremony marks the beginning of a new phase in your life. Perceive it as a new path ahead of you. The path starts with an insight into who you are. You will learn that you are a being of light," Niskala said. "Stand here please," Niskala helped her make a few steps in the dark, positioning Idolatra to where she should be.

"Repeat after me," Niskala said. Idolatra was waiting. She heard Niskala's steps, felt the movement of air, and sensed her perfume.

"Light is the joy of my life," Niskala said.

"Light is the joy of my life," Idolatra repeated, and a white point of light appeared from the darkness, above her, emitting a ray of light that landed on the top of her head. She felt a pleasant warmth. The ray continued to glow.

"Light is the attraction of our similarities," Niskala said.

"Light is the attraction of our similarities," Idolatra repeated, and the next ray, coming from a different point, a few feet in front of her, landed on her chest, continuing to shine.

"Light is my love that understands and protects others," Niskala said.

"Light is my love that understands and protects others," Idolatra repeated. Three rays of light, from the same point, landed on her; one on each shoulder, and one on her chest, continuing to glow.

"Light is my love that I give to myself," Niskala said.

"Light is my love that I give to myself," Idolatra repeated, and the next ray of light, from the same point, landed again on her chest, remaining there.

"Light is my compassion that I give to others," Niskala said.

"Light is my compassion that I give to others," Idolatra repeated, and a ray of light landed on her lower abdomen, continuing to shine.

"Light is my respect of our differences," Niskala said.

"Light is my respect of our differences," Idolatra repeated. A new ray of light landed again on her lower abdomen. It continued to glow.

"Light is my unique creativity, useful to all," Niskala said.

"Light is my unique creativity, useful to all," Idolatra repeated, and a new ray of light landed on her forehead, remaining there to glow.

"Light is the innocence of my inner child," Niskala said.

"Light is the innocence of my inner child," Idolatra responded, and three rays of light landed on her; one on each leg, and one on top of her head, remaining there to glow.

"Light is an incentive of my curiosity," Niskala said.

"Light is an incentive of my curiosity," Idolatra responded. Three rays landed on her; one on her forehead and one on each arm, remaining there.

"Light is the persistence of my hope."

"Light is the persistence of my hope," Idolatra repeated, and three rays landed on her; one on her forehead and one one each shoulder, staying there to glow.

"Light is my peace after forgiveness," Niskala said.

"Light is my peace after forgiveness," Idolatra repeated. Three rays landed on her; one on her lower abdomen and one on each foot, continuing to glow.

"Light is balance of how I live my life," Niskala said.

"Light is balance of how I live my life," Idolatra responded, and a ray of light landed on her forehead, continuing to shine there.

"Light is health of my body and mind," Niskala said.

"Light is health of my body and mind," Idolatra repeated, and a three rays landed on her; one on the top of her head, and one on each hand, continuing to shine.

"Light is Heliopolis!"

"Light is Heliopolis!" Idolatra responded. And the final ray landed on her forehead, continuing to glow there. All rays glowed together for a few more seconds, and then all vanished. Complete darkness filled the room.

"I am the light!" Niskala said louder.

"I am the light!" Idolatra repeated louder. She saw a genesis of tiny dots of light in her body, in her skin, in the locations where the rays had previously landed. The dots were trembling, slowly growing, becoming bigger and bigger. She thought she was dreaming.

"I am Heliopolis!" Niskala said even louder.

"I am Heliopolis!" Idolatra repeated it louder too. As she said these words, a myriad of light rays came out of her, and after those rays, more of them, and more. The light was incessantly being created from her being, emanating outward, filling the room, not leaving even an inch of darkness to reside in her. Her light did not flicker or fade; rays remained persistent, relentless and stable, and she knew that her light was not an ordinary light, but the one of her virtues. She shone on the floor and walls, on Niskala's smiling face and the rest of her body. Idolatra could see Niskala from every single light beam, and from their every angle, feeling that she was present in all of them, but also feeling that she remained in her body, firmly occupying it. She felt omnipresent in the room, filled with her indiscribable, unforgettable all-absorbing bliss.

The surface of the inner walls of the dome turned to a mirror, and Idolatra's rays multiplied even more, bouncing from it. Heliopolis was communicating with her; together they were creating light. Transparent spheres detached from the wall, changing their shapes into triangular prisms, and her every ray that entered the prism, refracted into a rainbow. Idolatra felt her life in each one of those colors, becoming aware of her immense inner beauty, embodying itself now in the external reality. All beauty of her virtues, that the Divine Source and Heliopolis imprinted in her soul, was manifesting now through the colors of this magnificent light.

"I am amazed at how much glorious beauty is in me," she said with happy tears pouring down her cheeks. "And at how much more there is in all of us," Idolatra hugged her sister, strongly feeling not only a deepening love for herself, but for the entire human race.

The walls of the dome scattered into spheres that quickly fused with Heliopolis, leaving only an open space where the dome stood. Idolatra's rays, moments ago confined within the dome, dispersed throughout the interior of the entire city, uniting with everything there was in it. Each dried flower petal touched by Idolatra's light, became fresh and alive, and each damaged tree branch regenerated.

She saw Niskala from every part of Heliopolis, from its every droplet of dew on every plant, from each rose petal, each leaf on every tree, everyone's clothes and skin, from eyelashes and faces. She became one with Heliopolis. Niskala was smiling, enjoying the purifying change that her sister was feeling.

From every single detail of Heliopolis, and from all perspectives, Idolatra saw herself standing, on the balcony, with her wings still spread... She looked like an angel... And as that thought crossed her mind, in that very instant, her wings retracted. She understood... Heliopolis was waiting for her to come to that realization, that she attained a higher level of existence, that she overcame her past and became someone embraced by the glory of light, someone who can help others accomplish the same.

"The retraction of your wings, concludes the ceremony," Niskala said. If you like, you can choose your new name as a symbol of your new beginning. Whenever you are ready for it."

"Yes, I would like that, very much," Idolatra responded.

"When you decide, let me know, and we will call you by your new name instead," Niskala commanded the spheres to build the dome again, getting ready to leave the tower with her sister.

"I already know," Idolatra, said, surprising Niskala. "I'd like my new name to be Rea, from the ray of light."

"So be it, then, Rea," Niskala said with a smile. She firmly hugged her sister, who equally hugged her back with a smile on her face.

...

That evening, after the ceremony, Rea visited Nora and Io in Niskala's castle. After she read them a good night story, Nora asked, "Auntie, how did you choose the wrong path in life? What happened?"

"Tell us, tell us," Io was curious too.

"That's a long story, my children," Rea said, with tears in her eyes. She looked at Niskala, asking her, without saying a word, if she would allow this topic. Rea was afraid of scaring the children or driving them away from her.

"If your aunt wants to tell you a story about that, and if she is ready, she can go ahead," Niskala said.

"I will probably not remember this story in a few days anyway, so I better tell you the story now. This is how it goes," she said, touching the noses of Io and Nora. "Once upon a time, when there were no telephones, nor video games, nor television, nor cars, nor money, nor states, nor kings, nor queens, and when men hunted and women gathered fruits and vegetables and stayed with children, I lived with my parents and sister Niskala, who was just a baby. The first ten years of my life, I had a different name though."

"A different name? Really," Nora interrupted, "how come?"

"What was your first name?" Io asked.

"My name was Kora." Rea said. "My father, Ezra, was a very unusual man…"

...

A black car was moving on a serpentine road along the coast of a large, beautiful lake. The driver was Jeremy, dressed in a suit and tie, wearing sunglasses. He arrived to a relatively small cemetery, located on an off-road, garden-like plateau facing the lake.

He parked the car and walked through the tombstones. He stopped next to one and removed his sunglasses. On the tombstone it read:

> Ashley McAllister, Ph.D.
> Dean of Philosophy Department, Princeton University
> (1993-2074)
>
> Here rests our beloved mother and grandmother.

Jeremy ran his fingers over her name. He pulled out an envelope from inside his jacket, opened it, took out a letter and placed it on the tombstone. Over the letter, as a weight, he put a glass bottle of perfume, which read, "Ashley." Then he walked back towards his car. The letter read:

"Dear Ashley, I have been feeling a very strong connection with you as of a few days ago. Something in me changed recently, and I kept remembering how we met and what we talked about… It was the Library of Alexandria… Now I admire it just as you always did, but it wasn't always like that for me… In fact, I was the one who issued a command to burn it... Then, I was blind, but now I can see. With this new heart beating in me, you and I would live happily, making our fragrances. Just as you wished many years ago. If only I could see your face again. Yours, Jeremy."

He stopped at a nearby intersection, noticing two cars that recently collided. An accident. The cars were still smoking, and the horn was stuck, making that horrible noise associated with accidents. He turned off his car and exited. Walking in a hurry to the accident scene, he called the police, reporting what he saw. A fire had just broken out on the hood of one of the cars. He quickly went to that car and removed a child, carrying it to a green pasture, away from the road. He touched the child's pulse, whispering: "Stay with me. You'll be fine." He went back and pulled out an adult's body, a woman, lying her next to the child. The woman was moaning in pain. The fire was getting bigger. He went to the other car, and pulled out one more body, an adult male. He lay the man's body on the ground in the pasture, next to others, and made one last trip to the car, retrieving from it a teddy bear and a children's book. As he exited the car and turned towards the pasture where the bodies were, the car exploded, and the flames engulfed Jeremy…

He woke up in a hospital, in bandages, with stitches on his forehead and arms. A nurse opened the door. Jeremy looked at her, completely surprised. In her face, he saw someone he thought he lost forever--she looked just like Ashley.

"Good day, Mr. Owens. My name is Alexandria, and I will be your nurse."

"Nice to meet you. You can call me Jeremy," he said.

"It's a miracle you survived. It must be a reward for saving lives yesterday," she was distracted by something on the table next to his bed, one of his personal possessions—a bottle of cologne. She approached it.

"Is this 'Ashley'?" She turned it and saw the label. "I thought so. My favorite." She uncapped the bottle and inhaled. "For some reason, it always reminds me of a toy store, but I have no idea why, though." She laughed. Jeremy could not believe how intuitive she was.

"Alexandria, how did you get your name, if I may ask?"

"My parents gave it to me," she said playfully and laughed, then added: "Actually, it was my grandmother… she admired the ancient Library of Alexandria; it was the best place in the world to her. She thought it would be a good name for me, and my parents agreed. What's your favorite place in the world?"

"Niskala's Heliopolis. I heard amazing stories about it. I haven't been there yet, though."

"You haven't? Well, you must! Perhaps we can visit it sometime together—after you heal, of course."

"I'd love that. I'd be honored," he said, and she sat next to him.

"It's unbelievable what you did yesterday. You are a true hero," Alexandria's eyes sparkled.

"Yesterday yes, but it wasn't always like that. I hope Heliopolis will take away centuries of tormenting memories and nightmares."

"It certainly will. But, what do you mean?" She took his hand into hers. Feeling a touch of her compassion, Jeremy then did what he thought was the right thing to do.

ACKNOWLEDGEMENTS

I'm very thankful to my editor Lisa Goddard-Fitzgerald who found time to work on my novel in addition to her numerous obligations. I also would like to express my deep gratitude to my wife, Ana, and my eight-year old daughter, Kim, who, for months, many hours per day, saw me working on my laptop, and did not complain. Kim only once said: "Dad, I will not invite you to my wedding." I said: "Why sweetheart?" "Since you will be working on your laptop." She responded. I am also thankful to Ana for providing valuable feedback on my writing.

Many thanks to Laurie Moore and Sterling Spector for providing me with their constructive criticism, edits, and incredible sensitivity for detail and the aesthetics of written expression. I am also thankful to Jeremy Lawrence who has polished my various novel-related writings. I must express my gratitude to my mother, Mila, for her enthusiasm for my work and constructive criticism, and my father, Vladimir, for helping me with the graphic design of the book's covers. Many thanks to Ingram Sparks, which allows authors to print their books on demand, and distribute their work both nationally and internationally. I am thankful to Wasif Bhatti for professionally formatting my novel.

Special thanks to shutterstock.com, where I obtained the images for my cover pages, and to the following artists (from the aforementioned website) whose work is featured on my cover pages: 4Max (image 345280676), Alexaldo (image 261033303), General-fmv (image 175521992), Christopher Ewing (images: 2880704, 2401515, 2390163, 46106932, 45125437, 46265596).

AUTHOR BIOGRAPHY

Iskar D'Abrel holds a B.S. degree in psychology (Texas Christian University, 1992), and an M.A. degree in biological psychology (San Diego State University, 1998). He worked (1998-2001) at the VA Medical Center, La Jolla (California) conducting research in the fields of Alzheimer's disease, Parkinson's disease, schizophrenia, bipolar disorder and depression. After working as an adjunct faculty at

Photo by Susan Manzoor

community colleges in the San Diego area (2001-2004), he became a full-time psychology faculty member at Long Beach City College (2004). He published a textbook in biological psychology in 2016, and a textbook in introductory psychology in 2017. As a writer of fiction, he has published three novels: *The Starfish Follower* (2015), its sequel *Heliopolis* (2017) and its sequel *Beyond the Wheel of History* (2018). In all of his novels he proposes ways to improve ourselves as individuals, so we can have a better human society.

WHY DID D'ABREL BECOME AN AUTHOR?

During Iskar's undergraduate education as a psychology student, he began to understand the human mind. At that time (1990s) his native country (the Former Yugoslavia) was going through a devastating war among ethnic groups that lived peacefully before. As a psychology student, he utilized what he learned from courses and textbooks, and he wrote essays trying to explain the madness happening in his homeland, as well as trying to offer ways of how to overcome it. Those written reflections about his native country plagued by war led him into thinking more globally about how to help human civilization work to change into a more humanistic world. So, his humanistic orientation as a writer of novels arose from the darkness of the human fall. As an author, he emerged from the ashes of war, from its absurdity, from human suffering, from prejudice, from discrimination. Even back then, when he was 22 or so, his orientation was crystal clear to him, just as it is now— he is a writer who proposes certain ways that we can use to change into better people so that we can turn the world into a better place.

His novel *The Starfish Follower* argues that reaching for our inner-child can enrich us with positive thoughts and feelings, which can improve our lives. His novel *Heliopolis* argues that our personalities can be significantly improved (morally, creatively, socially, intellectually, spiritually, physically and emotionally) if we are exposed to a center (Heliopolis) that integrates various activities, some of which are: parental education, proper nutrition, physical exercise, live music, live dancing performances, religious tolerance, massage therapy, as well as reaching for our inner-child, learning mental exercises for improving our mood, learning compassion, self-love, art-appreciation and relaxation in the Heliopolis' parks, jacuzzis and pools.

His novel *Beyond the Wheel of History* argues that an ultimate evil can be transcended by changing it into goodness. A divine intervention is needed for this difficult task, and it can be induced through followers of various different world religions genuinely uniting in mutual respect and cooperation.

He is currently working on a new novel, *The One That I Am*, which argues that it is essential to discover our life's purpose or mission as individuals, and to follow that path. Failure to do so may result in confusion, alienation from self and others or even illness.

www.iskardabrel.com

CPSIA information can be obtained
at www.ICGtesting.com
Printed in the USA
LVHW080529171118
597353LV00010B/119/P